# Women Without Fear
## *Men Without Tear*

by Gregory Kelekian

Published by Modern Legacy Solutions
Editing assistance provided by
bookmybio, Lawton, Oklahoma

ISBN 978-0-9950807-0-6
©2014
Canadian registration number 1117826

bookmybio.com

# Foreword

This book is not a biography, nor it is intended to be, but it is based on actual events. It shows the horrors that women are suffering in the Middle East, that these horrors are not confined only to the Middle East, that such abuses can and do happen here in North America and that evil should be denounced and challenged wherever and whenever it shows its face.

It tells the story of two women on two different continents and the humiliation and the abuses they suffered, but it also tells the story of friendship and how pain is felt by all.

At the beginning I didn't want to write it, but recent civil wars in the Middle East and the barrage of gruesome videos compelled me to tell my story. It is not a pretty story, but it is an important story that I felt needed to be told.

Some of the proceeds from this book will go to a charitable organization, an orphanage in the Middle East, and I dedicate it also to my wife, who growing up suffered abuses in her native country.

— Gregory Kelekian
March 1, 2016
Toronto, Canada

# Chapter One

Her green eyes looked at his with a mixture of pleading and determination. It was the determination that he hated so much. If only she would beg, submit, acquiesce in the presence of a man, he wouldn't be so angry. But it was there, still in her eyes, the independence, the energy that he so despised in a woman. So he shot. Immediately the eyes widened involuntarily, then they drained, the pleading but also the confidence and will. He was pleased.

He didn't know, couldn't have known, that her name was Foziah, couldn't have known that she was one of the most promising students in computer science at the technical college, couldn't have known that she was the spokesperson for whatever class or cause she was involved in, that she loved the color silver, that she had a quiet, persistent way of seeing her goals met.

Then the eyes dilated. Then he became aware that he was supporting all of her 110 pounds with his left hand, so he let her drop.

There is something that happens at the moment of death, especially a violent, unexpected death such as this one, that most people can feel in the pit of their stomach, a feeling of loss, not just of a person, but of a power in the room and in the world. But the gunman couldn't feel it, so he simply moved on to other rooms, seeking victims to satiate his incurable rage.

After he exited the student lounge in which he had taken the determination out of Foziah's green eyes, another man entered. This man, a man named Abraham, had faintly heard the gunshots on the floor below his office where he served as a computer science instructor at the Wilson Valley Institute of Technology, a small but, in its way, prestigious college in the far western suburbs of Boston. At first he thought it was some experiment gone wrong, some computer hardware exploding under the pressure of some prank the students were always playing. But then he felt a feeling in the pit of his stomach that told him it was something more. It was a feeling he had not felt for three decades, since he left Lebanon. He rushed downstairs into the student lounge.

He could not have been prepared for what he saw — Foziah lying in a crumpled mass, those green eyes staring at nothing and with none of the spark he was so accustomed to seeing in them. He pleaded with Foziah that that determination might return to those eyes. He pleaded with her to hang on. He dialed 911 but only got a busy signal. He tried to perform CPR but he was, as he always had been in anything important in his life, ineffective. The hateful bullet had done too much damage. He was unable to save the life of his star pupil.

He continued to hear gunshots down the hallway in classroom after classroom. He knew there was more to be done but he knelt petrified and paralyzed next to Foziah's body. Male students began running into the lounge, saying that the gunman had charged into classrooms, demanding the male students leave and the female students stay behind. One male student had stood in defiance of the gunman and been shot down. No one else dared be so bold.

The thought was at first hard to digest, but then it began to take shape in Abraham's mind. Women. He's targeting women. Then the unthinkable overwhelmed his consciousness.

"Mary!" At first it came as a whisper, barely escaping his lips, but he repeated it, with an urgency that pushed fear from mind and body. MARY! He screamed as he began running down the corridors toward the classroom where she taught.

His steps synchronized with the pounding of his heart as he surged toward the classroom at the corner of the sunlit hallway. As he turned the corner toward her room his eyes had to adjust to the darkness inside. Chairs were scattered. He nearly toppled over as he stepped in the room and skidded on the blood that seemed to cover every tile on the floor. There were three bodies lying motionless. He scanned toward the front and saw what he feared most. A familiar form, an outfit he thought he'd seen before, but her head was facing away from him, toward the exterior wall.

"Dear God. Dear God. Don't be her, please not her!"

He rested gently on his knees. He reached out. One hand on the shoulder, one on the top of the head. "Please God. NO!" He turned her gently, gently. No prayers today were to be answered. "Mary! NO!"

He sobbed. Over his incompetence, over his impotence, over Mary who had fallen victim to the angry bullet of a hate-filled man. At this moment he hated that he was a man, that he had something in common with the monster that had taken away the brilliant mind of Mary and the promising future of Foziah and, God, what of the others lying all around him.

Suddenly, as he cradled Mary's head in his hands, his mind raced back 30 years. He was looking at another body, another lifeless face that once lighted up a room. For a moment he wasn't sure if this was 1976 or 2006, if this was Mary he was cradling or Leyla. He couldn't save any of them — Leyla, Foziah or Mary. In that moment he wanted to die, too, to be executed for belonging to this miserable race.

# Chapter Two

Beirut, 1974

Abraham was born in Beirut, Lebanon in January 1955 . He was a privileged child.

His father worked as an investment manager for the Beirut branch of the Bank of Paris. His mother, Maya, loved to sew and sometimes did alterations to keep herself occupied, but mostly stayed home and raised her son, who listened to Jimi Hendrix and The Beatles on the record player in his room and drove a beat-up Austin Cooper up and down the side streets of his neighborhood. He liked to smoke cigarettes and dine with his friends at the Italian sidewalk cafe at the base of the condominium complex in which his family lived in. He enjoyed reading Kahlil Gibran and Truman Capote.

If there was a place ever created for the sole purpose of situating a city, it was Beirut.

The hills of the eastern suburbs rose like the seats of an amphitheater, affording lovely views of the world's largest sea. In Arabic, it was called al-Baḥr al-Mutawassiṭ, "the middle sea," and to Abraham it did seem to be in the middle of the world. Almost immediately due west from his home he could see the giant cargo ships navigating toward the port of Beirut and to the south he could see the flight lines of jumbo jets heading to and from Beirut International Airport.

Abraham's home in Broumana overlooked the sea from a vantage-point about 3,000 feet high. Sometimes in winter he would go with friends in the morning to Faraya, a mountain resort area some 6,000 feet above the sea. He loved the feel of the stinging cold and the freedom that came from sliding down the slope at 50 or 60 kilometers per hour. And unlike many other things in his life, he thought he was good at skiing. At least he rarely fell. Sometimes the way he would navigate the slopes would impress the girls who occasionally came with them. On occasion, it would be warm enough that same day to go down to the seaside and visit the beach. He was especially fond of going to Long Beach, a club where, for a few Lebanese lira, you could lounge all afternoon with a friendly waiter bringing you beers and where the women

4

wore the latest styles in swimwear, a place where men played backgammon and smoked cigars while businessmen drank the finest wines of both France and Lebanon's own Bekaa Valley.

An evening was not complete without a drink or two at one of the clubs that lined the streets of Jounieh. Abraham loved to dance, but felt awkward if a girl asked him to dance. Music was an individual experience for him and he preferred to experience it alone, inside his head and within the confines of his own body, especially if it was a live band, of which there were many in Beirut of the '60s.

After returning home he was fond of sitting on the balcony outside his bedroom on the fourth floor of his building and watching the sun set over the Mediterranean.

As he watched the planes fly over the vanishing point, he imagined the people inside — businessmen, stewardesses, politicians, students, young men who were following after a foreigner with whom they had fallen in love — and he ached to be part of a world that he was as yet too young to fully participate in, to see the cities in the Americas and to revisit the cities of Europe to which those planes were going.

He had once been one of those young men on one of those planes. His father had thought it was a good idea for him to see some of Europe, and so allowed him to go with a youth group to tour France and Italy. It was on that trip that Abraham had lost his virginity to a French girl his own age whose parents had moved to Beirut just a couple of years before. The trip was a sort of homecoming for her and it was clear that she felt comfortable making out with him. As for Abraham, his palms became sweaty when he sat next to such a pretty girl on the plane, and his heart palpitated when he first put his arms around her, almost involuntarily, when she suddenly embraced him in the hallway of hotel they stayed at in Lyon.

"What? Haven't you ever made out with a girl before?" he remembered her asking. He was embarrassed to admit he had never so much as held a girl's hand.

"Um," he stammered.

"See-leunce," she declared while putting the soft fingers of her left hand over his mouth as the fingers of her right hand stroked his back. He strained to restrain his disobedient body from the first moment she touched him. She drew him into her room.

"What if one of the chaperones come?" Abraham was frightened out of his mind, secondarily of the stern chaperone who would no doubt send them straight back on the next flight — actually the next two flights, for they would not be allowed to spend time together if they were found out — to Beirut if she discovered their rendezvous. He was frightened first and foremost, however, of whatever was about to happen. While, like any youngster, he found it exciting, he felt a sort of incompetence around a girl that he never felt in any subject in school.

"L'avez-vous pas entendue?" she asked. "Didn't you hear? Silence!"

So he was silent. And so it happened that he lost his virginity. Had she not offered, insisted actually, he never could have asked. Of course, after all was over, he was satisfied, but he also felt awkward, as if this French girl was now supposed to take on some sort of role in his life. But she was not in the least awkward, and for the rest of the trip she hardly acted like anything at all had happened. It was sex he'd had for the first time, but not love.

And so it was as he watched the planes carrying lovers to distant locations, he ached to be one of those young men in love. As with most men — if we could call them men, because in this era, 17-year-olds in Beirut still could be called "boys" — girls were the hottest topic in those smoke-filled cafes. All of Abraham's friends regaled him with stories of their conquests. Some had regular girlfriends but others seemed to go from one woman to another and were quite open about the fact that they cared about nothing more than the shape of the body in their hands. Abraham enjoyed the company of women, especially older women. While the conversation of men was always clouded by ego and braggadocio, the talk of women was more down-to-earth, more practical, more sensible.

His one true love was discovered one day while being shown around his father's bank office. His father, Elias, was a quiet, self-assured man who entertained hopes that his son, who took after his own introverted ways, would follow his footsteps into the world of finance. But while the bank ledgers and talk of amortization and escrow bored him to no end, he was fascinated when his father unlocked the door to a machine that engulfed an entire floor of the Bank of Paris building.

Inside he found the blinking lights and spinning reels of the IBM mainframe that processed the banks transactions much faster than a thousand accountants could. The idea that holes punched in a card could code information that represented the wealth of a nation transported his mind to a world where mechanical logic ruled, rather than the whims of men.

As he lingered between the mainframe and the window that provided a view of the front parking lot, Abraham looked down and recalled that he had not seen Samir, the security guard who had never failed to give him with a friendly greeting. Abraham had fond memories of being given a candy cane when, as a 10- or 11-year-old, he had come to see his father before the Christmas holiday. He asked his father where he was. Elias paused for a second.

"You know. I haven't seen him for a couple of days," Elias said, somewhat ashamed that he had been so engrossed in business he had failed to take note of the absence of a trusted employee. That was quite out of character for Elias, who prided himself on knowing the name and circumstances of all employees in his oversight, from the top executives to the lady who cleaned the toilets. He handed out money to employees at Christmas and Ramadan. When Elias returned to his office he asked his secretary, another longtime loyal employee.

"Oh, he's been home for the last two days," she said. "You know he's been laboring with his back for months. Well, it finally gave completely out on him."

"Would you please pull his personnel file?" he asked.

With any other boss, such a question could be ominous, a prelude to a termination, but Elias' secretary had no doubt that her boss was merely looking for Samir's address so as to provide some succor. He was not surprised to find that the address was in the Shia section of West Beirut.

Elias paused in front of the nine-story building in which Samir lived and rechecked the printout that showed the number of his apartment. He felt relieved that he would only have to climb five flights of stairs to get to his employee's flat. Elias never failed to appreciate the small favors life had paid him that enabled him to live in a building with an elevator.

As he mounted the final step and approached the door that opened onto the fifth floor hallway, he gathered himself and pulled his white cloth handkerchief out and wiped his forehead. He stepped through the door and took a moment to let his eyes adjust to the windowless passageway. He could hear the chattering of families in some apartments and the noise emitted by TVs in others. He finally located the correct number and knocked firmly, three times, on Samir's door. After about five seconds the door cracked open.

"Yes?" the woman on the other side asked tentatively.

"Yes, ma'am. I am looking to speak to Samir Hassan," Elias said, raising his voice just a bit to be heard over an argument echoing from the apartment behind him.

"And who are you?" was the suspicious reply that came through the barely opened door.

"My name is Elias Hajjar. I work at the bank with Samir."

"Oh," the door shut momentarily so as to unlatch the chain, then it swung wide open. "My apologies Mr. Hajjar. Elias has told me much about you. We are very sorry he has not come to work. I promise you he will come as soon as he is able."

"Ma'am. I understand that he is not feeling well. May I see him."

"*Habibti*, it is alright, let him come in." The words hardly sounded like they could have come from Samir, so slight was their effect, but Elias followed them through a door that led to a bedroom where Samir lay flat on his back.

"Samir, what is wrong?" Elias asked.

"Oh, boss, no worries. I will be back on my feet and at my post soon."

"Nonsense, tell me what is the matter."

"The doctor says I have a slipped disc in my neck. To be honest I can hardly lift my head."

"Then don't bother. I want you to take this," Elias pulled a card out of his wallet. "It is the name of a doctor who practices at St. George Hospital. Tell him I will pay all expenses related to your treatment."

Before Samir could utter a word of disapproval. Elias raised his hand to silence his employee.

"This is not a favor. This is an order from your employer. I cannot allow my best guard to go untreated. It is merely a business decision," Elias stated flatly.

It was, of course, not a business decision. But Elias knew exactly how a pill must be coated to coax a Lebanese man to swallow it.

A look of relief mixed with resignation crossed Samir's face. Through a slight smile he said. "Yes, boss. Thank you."

As he turned he saw the face that accompanied the tentative voice in the door, Samir's wife, in tears.

"*Shukran*. Thank you. Thank you so much, sir."

He looked at her straight in the face with a slight smile. "Nothing but a business decision. You have a good day ma'am."

When he arrived home, Maya was busily mending garments she

had taken in from the tailor shop of their neighbors, Arthur and Ani Zakaryan, a couple of Armenian descent whom the Elias and Maya had known for many years.

"Is there something the matter with Abraham?" Maya asked, peering over the spectacles she used for the fine details of stitching. "He looked more sullen than usual and went straight to his room."

Elias had almost forgotten the conversation he had with Abraham earlier in the day wherein he had tried to dissuade his son from a career in computer science. But the benevolent feeling that germinated in Samir's apartment had overtaken him.

He knocked on his son's door the moment he arrived home.

"Yes, father?" said Abraham, with his stereo headphones connected to his record player propped behind his ears.

"You want to study computers. I will allow you to study computers."

In some families such a declaration might elicit an embrace, but for Elias and Abraham, seeing each other eye to eye took the place of any physical contact and was a sufficient substitute for any declaration of gratitude.

Abraham would study computer science rather than finance when he was admitted to Beirut University. Elias was disappointed his son was not of a mind to follow him into his chosen profession, a profession that had allowed him to make a good life for his wife and son, but he also could clearly see that there was a future in computers — when he first came to work at the bank in the '50s everything was kept with pen and paper in ledgers, and that had all changed. Even his secretary had completely abandoned taking notes by hand and was typing everything out on electric typewriters.

And so it was that Abraham enrolled in the Computer Science program at Beirut University.

# Chapter Three

There is a certain dread that accompanies the first day at a new school, no matter whether you are a five-year-old tyke bustling off to learn your colors and alphabets or an 18-year-old attending college.

Abraham was affable and easy-going, but his introversion made making new friends difficult. After years of cultivating the same group of friends through his years of primary and secondary school, he hoped against hope that his new core of comrades would include someone he had known, even though none of his close friends had much interest in computers, thinking them the province of geeks. He had come to know many technically minded students in technology clubs and competitions during the last few years and he hoped he would find one in this classroom so he could latch on to an anchor of familiarity in this sea of novelty.

As he walked into the classroom, he first noted the instructor, silently gazing at leaf after leaf of scribbled notes. His tie was broad, after the fashion of the mid '70s, but that was the only thing stylish about him. His shirt was so wrinkled you imagined he had to have purposely retrieved it from the bottom of the clothes hamper. His thick mustache was disturbingly untended. When he looked up as Abraham entered the room, his enormous eyebrows almost hid his brilliant blue eyes, eyes that softened an otherwise care-worn face. Abraham nodded slightly and then turned his attention to his classmates, scanning quickly for any familiarities. Finally he saw a familiar pair of piercing blue eyes.

"Abdullah!" Abraham exclaimed, relieved to find an oasis of acquaintance.

"Abraham, you didn't tell me you were going for computer science."

Abraham had known Abdullah all his life. They and other electronics enthusiasts used to hang out at Kamal Shalloubs's electronics store to see the new gadgets and buy whatever they could afford. Kamal was a nice man and talked a lot about new and old technology and how technology was changing the world. He would give them a bag of Jordan almonds and tell them stories over a cup of tea.

He started toward a seat near Abdullah when his eyes met those of some young men whose demeanor gave him a sort of unease. They kept looking in one direction, and when Abraham looked there he understood immediately why.

There he saw what he'd never expected to see — a woman. At the moment he caught sight of her, he thought "ya salam welcome to the 20th century,"

Not that it was unusual to see a woman taking classes at Beirut University. Perhaps as many as a quarter of the students at the school were women, a percentage that had been growing every year. But technical trades like civil engineering and the maths and sciences were almost exclusively the domains of men, even in the West. And in a forward-thinking country like Lebanon, Abraham had never smelled perfume nor seen lipstick at any of the countless technology fairs he had attended throughout his high school days.

"Young man!"

Abraham had his back turned to the instructor when he felt these words strike him from behind. He had no doubt they were directed at him, so he turned about on his heels to face the teacher.

"Are you going to stand there staring all day, or are you going to sit down?"

"Yes, sir," Abraham was mortified. He wanted to remain anonymous and now he felt every set of eyes in the room beating down on him. He stumbled to the nearest seat. Fortunately it was directly next to a young man who, while not known to Abraham, had a face that felt familiar, a cool, self-assured look of the kind of guy Abraham liked to be around, given his own lack of certainty.

"Please listen for your name," wrinkled shirt called out.

The teacher, Abraham would later learn his name was Ahmed Musawi, called the names out one by one and by that means he learned the name of his new class companion — Raymond.

"Abraham Hajjar"

"Here"

"Excuse me, Mr. Hajjar, what did you say?"

At this point Abraham sat upright in his seat and looked straight at the disheveled instructor.

"I said 'here.'"

"Thank you," Ahmed said. "Please sit up straight and be alert. There's a lot you can miss in this class."

This clearly was not going well. But the discomfort was ameliorated by Raymond's knowing, mischievous smile.

"Leyla Jarred"

Abraham heard an audible sneer, uttering "haram!" — forbidden.

Leyla, who had been sitting upright in her seat the entire time, said "here," and it wasn't the cursory, apathetic "here" of a student avoiding an absent mark on an attendance register. It was the forthright "here" of a young woman announcing that she is taking a place in society to which she has an undeniable right.

In that moment it became clear to Abraham what she was up against.

In Lebanon, religion is an inherited culture, much as race in the United States. One doesn't decide to be, say, a white or black Southerner or a Brooklyn Jew. One just is. And that is the way religion is arrived at in Lebanon. You are a Christian or Muslim, not because you have a personal preference but because you came from a Christian family and you live in a predominantly Christian neighborhood. It was your identity regardless of your personal feelings about prophets or scriptures or even whether or not you believed in God. Religion was a fact of life, part of the landscape like palm trees and beaches. Like landscape, it was also something that was taken for granted by most, ignored by some, until some event, like a tree falling in a storm or a wave suddenly overtaking you, made the reality of Lebanon's religious divisions inescapable. That was what was happening in Beirut, and inside the computer science classroom at Beirut University, in 1974.

Abraham and his friends would come to refer to this group as "fanatics." In their minds, Leyla's presence in the class, learning how to program computers, the machines that everyone agreed were the future of humanity, was overturning the natural order of things. What most enraged the fanatics was that Leyla was a woman being trained to take control of her future, at a time in her life when they thought she should be home, under the control of her father until such time as he placed her in the control of her husband. But Leyla was clearly in control — a bright, educated, attractive if not beautiful woman who insisted on taking control of her own life, who was clearly intent on making her own decisions. Words cannot adequately describe how this fact infuriated the fanatics. Haram, indeed!

After class, several of the students — Abraham, Raymond, Abdullah and Leyla among them — decided to go to a pub that was a student favorite. As he entered the smoky, dark establishment, Abraham was taken aback when he recognized a group of seven people from his class in the back of the room, around a table that supported an open bottle of whiskey. Abraham, though from a Christian household, was surprised to see this group in a pub serving alcohol as it was 'haram' forbidden. In later years, Abraham would learn in his travels to the U.S. that hypocrisy was a trademark of religious zealots everywhere, be they Christian or Muslim.

The fanatics had clearly imbibed most of the whiskey as gauged by the volume of their conversation. One of them, who Abraham recognized as being named Marwan from the morning roll call, was drunker and louder than the others. As Abraham's group sat down and began pulling out their cigarettes, he could hear Marwan address the group at the next table.

"Do you think this is a proper place for women?"

They remained silent, trying to avoid eye contact, hoping he would go away.

"Did you hear me?" Marwan stood and began to walk toward the next table. "Do you think this is an appropriate place for a women to be? Because there's one right over there."

His drunken hand was unsteadily pointing in the direction of Abraham's group. Then his glazed gaze turned to Leyla. He stumbled toward them.

"Ya, sharmouta" a word which roughly translates to "whore."

No one said a word.

Then Marwan got more agitated and started swearing, then suddenly he took a knife out of his jacket pocket. To that Roger and Raymond who were sitting with Abraham took knifes out of their pockets to and yelled at Marwan to come and fight like a man.

Suddenly another one of the group who Abraham remembered was named Hussein, grabbed Marwan from behind.

Hussein was the smartest of the fanatics. He was the top performer in the class where most others, especially most of the other fanatics, were average or below average. Abraham always believed that he didn't belong with the rest of that savage bunch, and befriended him and tried to persuade him to change, even while keeping his distance from the rest of the group, much as everyone else did, Muslims and non Muslims. He believed this guy could be productive given his talents. Not only did he have a talent for computing, but he seemed to have a talent for life. He was a gymnast, a member of Lebanon's national gymnastics team, and as such traveled around the world for competitions.

"Come on Marwan," he said. "Let's not get arrested over this." The other five obediently followed as Hussein manhandled Marwan from the room.

"Are you OK Leyla?" Roger asked.

"Yes, of course," Leyla replied as she took calmly her seat and took a sip of the red wine she was drinking and slung her favorite possession, her light green Hermes bag down on the seat next to her.

Abraham was paralyzed, he never experienced anything like this in his entire life. His whole life he lived in an upscale community and went to private schools. He was living in a cocoon and suddenly he realized the reality of the streets in Lebanon. It was something his father wanted him to know. His father wanted him to go to a state university rather than a private one so that he experienced real life.

At the same time, Abraham felt ashamed, ashamed that he was a man, ashamed that he had not been the one to defend Leyla, ashamed at the fear he had felt in the presence of such drunken rage.

It would not be the last time Abraham would feel such shame.

# Chapter Four

Though it was Abraham's desire to throw himself into his studies, he could not know how futile this desire would soon turn out to be. The quiet rumblings that were going on outside Beirut University would soon explode and interrupt everyone's lives. Everyone's lives, of course, except for those who had interest in chaos and whose ideologies would fuel 20 years of death, despair and destruction. But there were a few moments for these students before their lives would be irretrievably changed, and in those moments, Abraham came to appreciate the acute mind and determination to succeed that Leyla possessed.

Being the only female in a classroom of men could be intimidating anywhere in the world. Being the only woman in a class of men in a technology class in Lebanon could be frightening, but being the only woman in a class that possessed fanatics who were violently opposed to the modern world and what that could mean for the modern woman should have been downright terrifying. But Leyla refused to be terrified. Abraham came to be deeply impressed by her quiet calm in the face of their sneers and subtle put-downs.

One day in April 1975, Abraham, Roger, Raymond, Leyla and Abdullah were unwinding after class at the same pub where earlier they had the confrontation with the fanatics when suddenly they heard excited voices and shuffling feet from the side of the bar where a small black-and-white television set was posted. The newsreader was solemnly dispensing something that was clearly quite momentous. Abraham could not hear exactly what was being said and could barely see anything on the minuscule screen.

"What's going on, George?" Abraham asked the man sitting on a stool closer to the set. George was someone that Abraham had come to know, a man who worked for about two years as his father's driver. He would often tell Abraham dirty jokes when Elias wasn't around, which was a thrilling experience for a 12-year-old. He held him in the sort of esteem juveniles sometimes have for adults of lesser intellect who, at 30, seem to be equals with someone who's 12 but, due to being 30, get to have the freedom of adulthood.

"I'm not sure, but I think those bastards killed Gemayel."

Those words sent a chill down Abraham's spine. As Abraham would later find out, they had not, in fact, killed Pierre Gemayel, the leader of the largest Christian political party in Lebanon. But they did kill four of his bodyguards and Abraham knew they had to get home immediately. The tensions they had felt inside the computer science class were just a shadow of the tensions that had been building all winter between the different factions. It was sure to explode now. The whole gang crammed into Abraham's Austin Cooper. It was imperative that they get home before the fighting started, but they already began to see young men, men the same age as Abraham, manning street corners with guns.

"Let me off. I'll walk home," Abdullah said.

"No way," Abraham replied. "You wouldn't stand a chance. I have to get you back to your neighborhood."

"Then you won't stand a chance."

"We'll at least get you to the edge," Roger said, adding a note of rationality to a moment that was quickly getting out of hand.

As they rounded the curve toward the Muslim quarter, Abraham noted a familiar face. It was Hussein. He had a machine gun and he was checking cars as they entered the Muslim neighborhood. He was the classmate who had intervened when Marwan was set to attack Leyla. In normal times Hussein was quiet, sensitive and, though as a gymnast he was muscular, he had a tender demeanor. Today he looked different for the first time.

He approached the passenger side of the Austin Cooper and leaned in.

"It's not good. You guys need to get home," Hussein quickly opened the door to let Abdullah out. "I'll make sure he gets home. There's been a shooting."

"I know, Gemayel," Abraham said.

"No, another shooting. Damn Phalangists murdered a whole bus full of Palestinian refugees. These guys are out for blood. Christian blood. Go home!"

Hussein slammed the door and Abraham hit the gas.

Abraham was driving 50 miles an hour on narrow streets in order to get home alive but all in the car knew there was more to the angry intensity of his driving than a simple desire to get home. Abraham realized he had been deceived by Hussein, even if at that moment he had saved their lives.

Hussein was shy and reserved, critical of many things the others were doing, a fact demonstrated by his defense of Leyla from being

16

assaulted in the pub. But now Abraham realized that at the critical moment, Hussein would take his stand with the militants.

At first they all thought their classes might never resume. For the next two weeks battles raged in the streets between militia groups and Abraham mostly sought refuge in his room, reading books he'd already read and listening to music to drown out the sound of explosions that were fortunately still relatively distant from his home. The weather this summer of 1975 was typically warm and humid, generally around 90 in the daytime and, though their flat was air conditioned, electricity was rarely on long enough to keep it cool. After the two weeks a temporary truce seemed to be reached and after two days of no fighting, the school phoned to say that school would begin again the next Tuesday.

He walked inside and noted that about half of the fanatics were in class, and they looked tired. Abraham had no doubt they had been in the thick of the fighting the last couple of weeks. Worst of all was Marwan. His eyes were bloodshot and seemed even deader than before.

The instructor, Ahmed Musawi, looked exactly the same as before the conflict — eyeglasses, uncombed hair, wrinkled shirt. Abraham smiled when he looked in the corner and saw Leyla. She gave him a quick smile back and she placed her beloved light green Hermes bag on the floor next to her seat. Abraham took his seat in front of Leyla.

"I am glad to see most of us made it back safely," Hassan said. "Now, if you'll take your books out, we will resume our discussion of PASCAL programming."

"Excuse me, Mr. Musawi," Marwan sneered. It took Abraham aback because Marwan was not in the habit of saying "excuse me" when he interrupted. "Will PASCAL help us learn to program missile guidance systems."

"I'm sorry sir, would you please get out your textbook," Hassan replied, with his glasses at the bridge of his nose and his eyes fixed on the book and away from Marwan.

"We shouldn't kid ourselves," Marwan insisted. "Very soon, all of us will be putting our skills to the test. This lull won't last long. We will all be joining the fight. We won't all be on the right side of the fight," as Marwan said these words, his eyes fixed firmly on Abraham, who felt the intensity of those eyes while his own were fixed on the open textbook before him. "But we, all of us, will be in the fight."

Hardly had Marwan finished his sentence, when the instructor slammed his book down on his desk. The sound wave thus produced startled Abraham and caused him to jerk involuntarily. As Musawi marched toward Marwan he pushed in glasses back up the bridge of his nose and lowered his face until is was level with Marwan's, Musawi's eyes flaring in anger, Marwan's half opened and cold, staring at the floor.

"Mr. Marwan if you want to remain in this class you will open your book and shut your mouth. If you do not, you may leave and you will never be welcomed back. Do you understand me?"

"Yes sir," Marwan said, barely opening his lips.

"Excuse me, what did you say?"

"YES," Marwan exclaimed as he raised his dead eyes to meet Hassan's, who in response straightened his body, now standing away from Marwan.

"Thank you," Musawi said. "And if the rest of your friends who didn't join us today would like to return, please tell them the same will apply to them."

The next day Hassan noted that Marwan was absent and he wondered, or perhaps wished, that he wouldn't return. He told Leyla.

"Oh, no, he'll be back," Leyla affirmed.

"What makes you so sure?" Abraham asked while Hassan's back was to the class as he wrote out PASCAL keywords on the chalkboard.

"He's here for a reason. He sees the conflict ahead. He's a Neanderthal, but he's not stupid. He wants to make a place for himself in the militia and computer science is his key to the future. It makes him not as expendable."

Leyla was, of course, right. She was always right. She could see, not just the exterior of people, but down inside their soul, their motivations, their fears. It made her interesting but it also made her frightening to lesser men, men such as the fanatics.

"What's that?" Abraham asked.

"What's what?"

"This," Abraham said while grasping at a peace of paper stuck inside a textbook with a red plus sign printed on the portion of the page you could see sticking out from the book.

"It's nothing," Leyla said, simultaneously snatching the book back toward her stomach. "Well, OK, I guess I can tell you. The Red Cross is starting a class — first aid, conflict resolution — the sorts of skills we'll need to make through what's ahead of us."

"Is there room for others to join?" Abraham asked hopefully.

"Really, Abraham? I didn't think it was your sort of thing."

"It's not. But if the smartest person I know thinks it will help us get through the next few years, I think I should take advantage of the opportunity."

The next three months an uneasy truce settled over the city, but settle it did, and after a few weeks Abraham began to believe that life might return to normal. After class he and Leyla would usually ride together to the Red Cross building in the center of Beirut, an area teeming with colleges and, therefore, students.

It was on those drives that Abraham would get lost in listening to Leyla. She was not the most intelligent girl he had ever met, nor was she the most beautiful. At 5-foot-4, with dark hair and brown eyes, there was nothing in her appearance that would make her stand out of the Beirut crowd. Nothing until she smiled. Abraham would often try to make a joke, a quick turn of phrase, a pun or a jab at one of their professors, for the sole purpose of evoking that subtle smile, a smile that created an atmosphere of contentment. When she was happy, Leyla had a look of serenity that the great medieval artists tried to create when they rendered the Madonna. But she had a calm determination, a quiet intensity that were mesmerizing to a man like Abraham, who was never quite certain what he wanted out of life. Leyla knew exactly what she wanted, to live life on her terms, not bending to the will of adults or society or the expectations of men, especially the narrow minds of those who belonged to the fanatics.

Her voice was soft but strong, articulate but not intimidating, tenacious but tranquil. She sometimes joked about sexuality, something rare in a woman in 1970s Beirut. Sometimes when she was in an ill mood she would blame her time of the month. All of this made her the kind of girl who felt at ease in the male-dominated world of the computer science class.

It was also during this time period that something happened at school that got everyone's attention. The computer lab was overseen by a man by the name of Joseph. On one occasion, as Abraham and Leyla were working together at a terminal that connected to the school's mainframe, Joseph walked by and stopped suddenly.

"You're still here?" he asked incredulously.

"Are you talking to me or Abraham?" Leyla responded.

"I really thought you were just trying to prove something. Why don't you transfer to a school more appropriate for you? Teacher's college, something like that?"

"Why don't you mind your own business?" Leyla stood up and was almost eye level with Joseph, who was short for a man.

"This class is my business. And I don't lower my standards just because someone thinks it's a good idea to let girls into computer science."

"Good thing Beirut University doesn't lower its standards for students the same way it has for teachers." You could now almost see fire sparking from Leyla's intense stare.

"Next week is the semester final. We'll see how confident you are then." With that, Joseph turned to walk away.

"*Ibn kalb*," Leyla said as she lowered herself back into her seat next to Abraham. "Son of a bitch."

"I don't think he's kidding," Abraham said, his eyes turned to the floor. "I've heard the first semester exam of the second year is the toughest. I've known several students who dropped out of the program after taking it."

"Well if I wasn't going to pass it before, I'm sure as hell going to pass it now. After Red Cross tonight we'll go back to your place for study," Leyla's confidence and dependence upon him as a study partner gave him an unspoken pride.

The test was harder that Abraham had imagined. It contained questions on some programming commands that he'd never heard of. It covered PASCAL as well as COBOL, the latter of which he had barely scratched the surface.

He looked over toward Leyla. Her eyes were fixed on her paper. He looked up and saw Joseph staring down at him. He turned his glance back down to his paper and struggled to finish by the end of class.

"That was harder than I expected," Abraham later told Leyla as they sat in Beirut traffic on the way to the Red Cross offices.

"Really? I feel pretty good. I didn't know all the parts about COBOL, but I think I did OK."

"You always think you did OK," Abraham sputtered as he jerked the car into second gear to spurt ahead.

"And I'm usually right," she said as they whirled into the parking lot.

That evening the subject was hostage negotiation, a subject that

Abraham found especially tedious. Abraham had never been a good student of human nature and this course was primarily about understanding the motivations of the brutes who would hold a human hostage. He didn't understand why people did such things to innocents and his only thought was that such people should be executed. But Leyla seemed especially intrigued by the subject and why not? She was, of all the people he knew, someone who was skilled at convincing others to do things her way. He figured she would be a fine hostage negotiator, should that day ever come.

The next day was the last day of class for the semester, and it wasn't really a day in class at all. All there was to do was to go to see the semester test grades posted on the classroom door. Abraham first scanned for his last name. Next to Hajjar, he saw the number "77." Not great, but not as bad as he had feared. He had passed. He would be able to take the second semester of the second year and then move on to his specialty.

He now looked for Leyla's name and was taken aback to see the word's "see professor." Leyla must have sneaked up behind him because as he turned around he looked directly at her face.

"Well, I guess I have to see *ibn kalb* face-to-face."

Most of the students had already left for the semester break when Abraham accompanied Leyla down the hall leading to Joseph's office. Abraham had never felt fearful in his school before, but something about walking with Leyla down this empty hallway, toward the office of an ignorant buffoon like Joseph and with the unseen menace of the student fanatics, perhaps not right here, but somewhere and everywhere in this tense city made Abraham anxious for Leyla. She was vulnerable in a way her fearlessness excluded her from understanding, and certainly made it impossible for her to hide from it.

"You should go. I'll be OK," she said as they paused in front of Joseph's office door.

"No, you shouldn't be alone here. It would not be proper." Propriety, of course, was not Abraham's strong suit, but it was the best reason he could come up with.

"Alright," she said with a sigh and her face lit up with that confident smile of hers. "You wait out here. This shouldn't take long. I'm sure it's nothing."

Abraham sat on a bench and Leyla knocked on the door.

"Come in."

21

Leyla opened the door and marched through, only halfway shutting it behind her, much to Abraham's relief, so he could hear much of the conversation that followed.

"You wanted to see me before giving me my grade." Leyla made this question into a statement.

"Yes, Ms. Jarred. Please sit down."

"That's OK, I'm sure it won't take long to gather my grade. I have to get to my Red Cross class, so if you will kindly give me my grade I will be on my way."

"I think you know why it can't be that easy. Would you please explain how you cheated on the exam?"

"I'm sorry. I must have misunderstood you."

"You understood me very well. Please explain how it is that you cheated on your exam. We all know you are at best an average student. But somehow you came away with the best mark, 90 percent. Was it Abraham? I saw you making eye contact with that boyfriend of yours." Joseph now flung his left hand in the direction of the half-closed door behind which Abraham stood.

"He is NOT my boyfriend. He IS my friend. He made a 77 on that test. I made a 90. How could I have possibly cheated off of him, or anyone for that matter if I got the best mark?" Abraham peeked around the corner just enough to see Leyla leaning across Joseph's desk, her face within striking distance of Joseph.

"I have wondered that myself. But if I have learned anything in my years of teaching is that when something is out of the ordinary, there's something behind it. This result cannot be allowed to stand. You will have to take the test over again."

"Fine," she straightened back up again. "I'll take this test over and over again, as many times as you'd like. Maybe one day you will get tired of making up allegations to cover for your own inadequacies as a teacher. It's a shame your teaching is so poor that the best mark was only 90 percent. And the only reason I got that was that I studied the book myself, without regard to your lectures."

With that Leyla slammed the office door behind her with such ferocity Abraham could hear items falling from Joseph's shelves.

"Aren't you afraid the next test will be harder?"

"Not really," Leyla said as she swung the door open to the parking lot. "I'm already better at coding than he is."

The next day Abdullah accompanied them as Abraham took Leyla back for the makeup test. Abraham was not allowed into the classroom, but Ahmed, their main instructor was there for monitoring.

"It'll be OK. Ahmed's a fair man. He won't let Joseph do anything against Leyla," Abdullah reassured Abraham.

"I guess so," Abraham said tentatively. "I just can't shake the feeling that Leyla is vulnerable. And it's like she doesn't know it."

"She knows it," Abdullah said as he shut the door after hopping into the passenger seat of Abraham's car. "She just can't acknowledge it. If she did, it would be like telling the world she shouldn't be here."

"Maybe we shouldn't be here," Abraham said as he cranked the car. "But Leyla ... Leyla can be anywhere she wants to be."

They drove to Abdullah's father's computer shop, a comfortable oasis from Abraham's childhood where he first saw many gadgets that set his young mind ablaze about the potential of technology.

"So, Abdullah tells me they made your friend Leyla retake the test," Kamal said as he placed the Jordan almonds in his hands and patted him on the head. "I wouldn't worry. She seems pretty smart. I say she'll do just fine."

The next day on the classroom door was posted a large piece of computer printout paper, the kind with green rows interspersed with white space on which a few days ago all the students' exam scores were posted. On this paper there was only one name, "Leyla Jarred," and only one number, "93." Beneath it, in Ahmed's handwriting, were the words "Congratulations. You win. *Ibn kalb* loses."

# Chapter Five

The beginning of the next school term was delayed by renewed fighting, this time more intense, more random, more deadly. Abraham and Leyla's training had been completed and now they spent every day tending the wounded, pulling elderly people and children — sometimes barely alive, sometimes dead — out of the rubble of shelled apartment buildings. Leyla had progressed further in her medical training than Abraham had, so she was more involved in tending the wounded at Red Cross field hospitals set up near hotspots.

About a week after Leyla's triumph over *ibn kalb* she and Abraham were walking toward one of the few pubs still open where they planned to meet friends in a quieter section of the city.

"You're pretty good," Abraham started after a long silence.

"At what?" Leyla crinkled her nose in doubt.

"Being a nurse. You're good with people. You think maybe when this is over you'll give up on computer science and become a nurse?"

"Oh, so you think I should move on to a woman's job."

"Oh, OK. I get it. So you could be a doctor."

"I could," Leyla said self-assuredly. "But that would be six more years of schooling. I'm getting tired of school. Maybe computer science isn't as fun as I thought it would be, but I'm close to graduating and I'm ready to live a real life."

At that moment they heard an explosion like none they had ever heard before. Soon afterwards, a fine dust enveloped them, the tell-tale sign that a building had collapsed.

As they rushed around the corner, they could hear moans and screams coming from the rubble. They saw the burning skeleton of a car.

"Car bomb," said Leyla. "They must have really wanted to kill someone here."

Abraham and Leyla joined about a dozen men moving pieces of concrete and pulling the wounded and the dead out. As Abraham was pulling jagged chunks of concrete out of the way, he heard to his left a dog's whining bark. At first he thought the dog might be injured but when he got to the area where the dog was standing he realized there was a young girl trapped beneath debris. He could now hear her faint cry. When he tossed aside a mass of roof materials he saw the girl, perhaps 12 or 13. He tried to pull her out but her legs were trapped by a large beam. He attempted to lift it but could not.

"Help me," she wheezed, her face white from the fine power that filled the air.

"There's a girl here. Help me get her out," Abraham screamed. A few men came but were unable to budge the beam. Abraham began to sense that feeling that had washed over him from time to time in his life, the overwhelming weight of his ineffectualness.

Leyla pushed through the group of men who were gathered around and leaned over the girl's body, placing her ear on the girl's chest.

"Not good," she said, her eyes narrowing. "Her breathing is labored. Her head wounds are too severe. I've seen this before. She could suffocate from the inflammation."

Leyla looked around until she saw a face she was looking for.

"Ismail!" she called out to one of the men who had come from the nearby Red Cross hospital tent, "Where is everybody? We need doctors and nurses."

There was a bombing on the other side of The Green Line," Ismail said, in reference to the street that separated the mostly Christian from the mostly Muslim section of Beirut. "We tried to send someone to fetch a doctor, but it may take awhile."

"Go get a tracheotomy kit and someone qualified to administer it." Leyla said this while moving into place two large timbers, wedging them underneath the beam on the girl's legs. Ismail turned and ran toward the Red Cross tent hospital.

"OK, I need three of you guys over here," she said, indicating the lever she had place to the right of the young girl, "and I need three of you on this one," indicating the lever to her left.

Abraham started forward but several much stronger men moved in front and positioned themselves to lift.

"OK, on the count of three!" Leyla placed her arms underneath the prone girl's armpits. "One! Two! Three!"

The men grunted in unison, raising the beam about half a meter, just enough for Leyla to pull the girl back.

"OK."

And the men dropped their load and the beam fell back to the ground, stirring up another cloud of the fine white dust.

About this time Ismail came racing back with a box in his hands and two men carrying a stretcher.

"These men aren't doctors," Leyla said as they approached.

"No one could even get back to the tent. Patrols are blocking the streets."

"So are you saying if we get her back to the tent there won't be a doctor or a nurse there either?"

Ismail merely shook his head as Leyla snatched the trach kit from his hands.

"I guess I'll have to do it, then."

"You've been trained in tracheotomies?" Abraham asked.

"I've watched."

Leyla knelt next to the girl and listened again to her chest.

"I'm not getting good breath sounds. I have to do this or she'll asphyxiate."

She tore open the box and unwrapped a long, slender needle. Abraham turned his head. He couldn't bear to watch.

"Don't just stand there Ismail, help me."

Ismail knelt down between Abraham and the girl and Abraham felt a bit of relief that his view was blocked even when he turned toward Leyla.

"OK. I'm in the trachea. Give me the tube," and a few seconds later she asked for the bag and he could hear Leyla pumping air into the girl's lungs through the incision in her throat.

"Here Ismail. Keep pumping."

Abraham looked over and could see Leyla listening again to the girl's chest.

"I hear breathing sounds. Get her on the stretcher."

The two men lifted the girl who was regaining color under the fine patina of white dust that covered her face. About that moment, several ambulances began to drive up. Evidently they had finally made it across The Green Line.

Abraham realized he had been a spectator in a moment of peril, that had it not been for Leyla taking charge, that girl would have died and Abraham would have been helpless to prevent it. As he wandered away from the building he pulled a cigarette from his pocket and lit it. The dog that had alerted him to the girl's plight silently followed him.

"You haven't ever smoked before!" Abraham was a bit shocked to find that Leyla had walked up behind him. He had been so lost in thought that he hadn't noticed her approach. She grabbed his arm and held it up so that she could take a drag off his cigarette.

"I haven't ever been in a war before," Abraham replied before putting the cigarette back in his lips.

"Hey, hold on, are you OK?" She grabbed his arm somewhat more forcefully this time, causing him to almost fall backward before coming to a stop.

"Why shouldn't I be OK?"

"I think you're embarrassed that you weren't able to get that girl out from under that beam. It took a half dozen men to do lift it. Do you want to be some sort of Superman?"

"I want to be some sort of man." Leyla's eyes widened and Abraham could tell his words had shocked her.

"You're just so much better than me under pressure," Abraham continued. "I'm not sure I should have even joined the Red Cross class. I'm not much use. I freeze up."

He took one last long drag from the cigarette and dropped it to the ground. And he lifted his foot to step on it Leyla's foot stepped on the butt.

"Come on," she said, once again grabbing his forearm. "You sound like you need a drink worse than I do."

As they walked along the dog continued to follow them.

"Go back," Abraham yelled into the German shepherd's face, at which the dog doubled back momentarily, but then continued following once Abraham turned around.

"Looks like you've got a new friend," Leyla said.

"I think maybe he is that young girl's. Now he doesn't have a home."

"I think he wants to come home with you to show his gratitude for saving his master."

"His master was a girl. Maybe you should take it until the girl recovers."

"Are you crazy? You've seen the apartment we live in. Where would we put a dog? My dad would kill me if I brought home a dog."

So Abraham took the dog by his house and deposited him in the yard on the way to the pub.

When they got to the pub, only Raymond was left waiting for them. The rest had gone home.

"What happened?" Raymond asked. "You're both bloody."

For the first time Abraham and Leyla realized that, along with the white dust, their clothes were also stained in blood, from the young girl and from the others they'd pulled out of the rubble.

"Leyla saved..." Abraham began, but Leyla cut him off.

"You should have seen Abraham. Such a hero. There was a car bomb and he leapt right in. Saved a 12-year-old girl's life by pulling her out of the rubble."

"Well then a drink for my friend," Raymond said to the bartender. "A least someone is a hero in this mess."

The next day Abraham had determined he would not be going in to the Red Cross office. He was emotionally drained from the previous day and wanted to sleep in. The phone rang downstairs and his mother came up to say it was for him.

Annoyed, he went downstairs. If it was the Red Cross he was thinking of telling them he was finished with them for good.

"Abraham, we need you down here," came the voice over the receiver and before he could protest the voice continued, "there's been a kidnapping, actually two kidnappings, and one of them is Kamal Shalloub."

Abraham could hardly believe his ears. Mr. Shalloub was a kind and generous man, so generous, in fact, that he wasn't a wealthy man.

"Kidnappers couldn't possibly think Mr. Shalloub's family could pay much in ransom."

He told the man, whose voice he recognized as Simon, one of his instructors in the hostage negotiation course, as much.

"They don't want money. They want a pawn."

He explained how that morning the Phalangists, the Christian militia, took Mr. Shalloub hostage because he was a Muslim, this in retaliation for the Lebanese Arab Army, the Muslim militia, who had taken a Christian man hostage. They wanted a swap. They had sent Faisal to negotiate with the Muslim militia for the life of Christian man.

Abraham recognized Faisal as the name of one of his hostage negotiation classmates whose father was an engineer and a factory owner. This is what it had come to. Abraham realized his worth to the Red Cross came from the fact that his father was a prominent businessman in the Christian community, just as Faisal's was in the Muslim community.

"I'll be right down," Abraham said, and lowered the receiver into its cradle slowly, still shocked that anyone would want to harm such a harmless man as Mr. Shalloub.

28

"You can't go. It's too dangerous." Abraham had almost forgotten his mom was standing there but was awakened to her presence by the strenuousness of her objection.

"Mom, I have to go. It's Mr. Shalloub."

"I don't care if it is Jesus Christ himself. There is no sense in both of you getting killed."

"Mom, they won't touch me. They respect *Abi*," Abraham said, using the Arabic word for "Papa." "That's why the Red Cross is sending me. They know I have the best shot at freeing him. I have to try."

He reached around his mother to give her a hug and he could feel her stiffen in fear.

"Maybe all those hours of training will finally do some good."

He put his arms on his mother's shoulders, still stiff, and eased her into her chair.

"I'll call you when it is all over."


The place where Mr. Shalloub was being held was a 10-story apartment building near the Green Line which had been cleared of all residents and was now being used as a field office by the Christian militia. Just down the street the Red Cross had set up its hostage negotiation efforts. Simon was standing behind a desk that had been requisitioned for this purpose and held some of the manuals that had been studied during the course and a bullhorn.

"Abraham, I see you've dressed for the occasion," Simon remarked.

Abraham hadn't thought about what he was wearing. He had on the Coca-Cola T-shirt he had put on that morning, thinking this day would be just as boring as the one previous.

"Listen," Simon continued, "one of the reasons we chose you is that the leader of this brigade is George. We know he worked for your father."

George. The man on whose lap he had once sat. The man who told him dirty jokes with a wink just as he was entering manhood. Though he was momentarily shocked, he was not surprised that George would be part of the Christian militia and taking a revenge hostage. His personality, though affable, always had a whiff of inhumanity about it.

"I will be coming with you and so will Peter," Simon said, nodding to the man who had escorted him in, a man he'd never seen before.

"What about Leyla?" Abraham asked.

"Who?" Simon responded with a puzzled look on his face.

29

"Leyla. She has a way with people. I think this would be a good job for her.

"Leyla," Simon said matter-of-factly, "is a girl. This is no place for a girl."

"Then why did you let her take the class?"

"As you said, she does have a way with people. I couldn't refuse her, but I knew there was no way we could ever use her here."

Abraham knew further objections would be futile, but he also knew that his efforts would likely also be futile. He had never been good at convincing anyone to do anything; he didn't have Leyla's easy confidence. That familiar feeling of incapability began to wash over his body again. Abraham was so ineffective that he couldn't even succeed in bringing the one person in who, he felt, could save Mr. Shalloub's life.

Simon grabbed the bullhorn off the desk and beckoned Abraham and Peter to follow him. They walked the several blocks down to the hostage building. A man with a Kalashnikov hanging from his neck put up his hand.

"Captain Kouri says he only wants to talk to the kid," he said, pointing the Kalashnikov at Abraham.

"That's not the deal," Simon protested. "I told George we all go in ..."

His words were cut short by a sudden burst from the Kalashnikov. Abraham immediately fell to the ground, his hands over his face. After about three seconds, Abraham realized he had not been hit. He looked behind him and both Peter and Simon stood staring back as Mr. Kalashnikov. The gun had shot over their heads.

"He comes alone or no one comes," the man said.

"I'll go," Abraham said, trying to mask the terror welling up inside him. "It's the least I can do for Mr. Shalloub."

"What were you trying to pull? I know your friend Peter. He's no Red Cross worker. He's regular Lebanese army," Mr. Kalashnikov said as they mounted the stairs to the third floor.

"He's not my friend," Abraham retorted.

They entered a room lit from outside by sunlight that invaded the room through broken windows. A small fan whirred in the corner, providing little relief to the still heat inside the space.

George walked in from an adjoining room.

"Abraham, so good to see you. So sorry it had to be under these circumstances."

"George, what are you doing? Mr. Shalloub never hurt anyone."

"I know. And it hurt me to take him hostage, but he was the only Muslim we could find. If you convince the Muslim militia to release their hostage — he is a good man, too — Kamal Shalloub will be a free man."

"Let me see him first so that I can assure them he is unharmed."

"Help yourself," George said as he stepped aside.

Abraham walked into a secondary room, even hotter and darker than the main room, and in the corner sat Mr. Shalloub with his hands bound behind his back and Mr. Kalashnikov standing guard over him.

"Abraham," he said in a feeble voice, "I didn't expect to see you today. I must apologize that I have no almonds with me."

"Mr. Shalloub, are you hurt in any way?"

"Oh, no. My hosts have been almost impeccable in their hospitality, except that these ropes are a little tight on my hands."

Abraham turned to Mr. Kalashnikov, "Let him loose. You're not afraid of an old man are you?"

"Does the Red Cross teach all their hostage negotiators to be so demanding?" The voice was that of George, behind him in the entranceway to the small room where Mr. Shalloub was held hostage.

"Why tie his hands? There's no way for him to escape," Abraham turned and protested to George.

"You are right Abraham, there is no way for any of us to escape," and with a short pause and sigh, he nodded to Mr. Kalashnikov, who produced a knife to cut the old man's hands loose.

Mr. Shalloub stood as Abraham walked toward him. He set his hand on Abraham's head.

"My dear boy. You are such a man now. You must make me a promise. If this doesn't turn out the right way, you must tell Abdullah my last thoughts were of him."

"Mr. Shalloub ..."

Abraham was interrupted by a raised hand and a "tisk, tisk, tisk."

"You must listen to your elders, while we still have the ability from Allah to speak. I have learned through many years that difficult situations often end badly. Many years of suppressed hatred and bad decisions have led us to this day. I am not afraid. I trust that the next life will be more peaceful than this one. I only worry of my family who must deal with this one."

"I'll get you out of here Mr. Shalloub. You can tell Abdullah yourself."

Mr. Shalloub patted Abraham on the chest twice. "Good, you must try. But if it turns out badly you must promise not to blame yourself."

Abraham saw in Mr. Shalloub's eyes a sort of light he'd never seen before, something akin to liberation. He halfway wondered if this man looked forward to the worst outcome. But it was an outcome that Abraham was not prepared to accept.

Abraham stepped back from his mentor a couple of paces, then whirled around on his heels and walked with determination toward the Red Cross' two-way radio.

"Faisal, are you there?" Abraham shouted into the radio.

"Yes. It's difficult. The commander is very angry. There was an attack last night and his family were all killed."

Abraham's heart sank at this news. A man with nothing left to live for has nothing left to do but to kill and die. Abraham tried to think quickly. He reflected on his situation, grasping at anything he could think of.

"Abraham, I'm afraid we do not have much time. The commander is getting more and more agitated."

"I have an idea. Let me speak to the Muslim militia commander." Abraham's eyes were alight. He had struck upon an idea. It was one of those sad notions that comes from a place of defeat, but it was at least a way to save Mr. Shalloub's life.

"Yes, you asked to speak to me," barked a hoarse voice through the radio.

"Listen," said Abraham into the radio, trying by force of will to keep his voice at a reasoned pitch. "I know you are angry. The Christians took your family and you want to take revenge."

"*Insha'Allah*," came the response. If God wills.

"OK, you are right. A price must be paid. But must that price be at the cost of the life of your Muslim brother."

"There are many martyrs and there will be many martyrs. I cannot stop the cycle of martyrdom."

"But you can spare the life of your brother and still avenge the blood of your family. Listen to me. You may cut off the right hand of your captive."

"What the bloody hell are you talking about?" George bounded across the room toward Abraham with incredulity on his face. "What kind of negotiator are you?"

Abraham covered the microphone. "One who gets his captives out alive."

"Are you there commander?" Abraham had taken his hand off the mouthpiece and was restating his deal. "If we cut off the hands of our captives, then your family will have been avenged. We will have shed blood. But you will not be a murderer."

The pause seemed to stretch into minutes though it was only a few seconds. Finally, on the other end he heard, "OK."

He could hear a command barked out on the other side of the transmission. Faisal now had control of the radio.

"A soldier has a machete and is heading toward the hostage," Faisal reported. "Red Cross home base, have the medics ready with an amputation kit."

"This is Red Cross home base, roger!" came the response from the third party that until now Abraham had forgotten was even listening.

Then he heard a blood-curdling scream. This was expected. What came next was unexpected. There were shouts of confusion. He could hear a mass of footsteps over the radio.

"Faisal, Faisal, what happened?

"Um ... sir ... um ... nothing happened. There was a bit of a struggle but the hand is off."

Abraham looked at George and said, "Your turn. You know you don't have to do it."

George looked at him with eyes that were both amused and empty.

"You're very smart. You know I have to do this."

He turned to Mr. Kalashnikov and told him to find his machete.

At that moment an excited voice came over the radio.

"Commander Kouri! Commander Kouri!"

Kalashnikov stopped his search and looked up at George.

"Yes, comrade. What is it?"

"The hostage, they had tied his right hand, but with his left hand he grabbed the sword from the soldier and he pushed it into his own stomach. The hostage is dead."

Abraham felt numb.

"No!" he shouted. "This hostage chose this path for himself. Don't punish Mr. Shalloub." Abraham had flung himself to his knees, pleading with George.

"This is not punishment. This is war," George said coldly. "You were always a foolishly naive boy."

George then turned and nodded to Kalashnikov, who thrust aside the machete he had found and pulled the rifle forward from his neck.

"NO!" Abraham screamed and flung himself from his prone position before George toward Kalashnikov. With just a flick of Kalashnikov's wrist, he brought the back of the rifle smashing into Abraham's forehead. Abraham crumbled to the floor in the doorway of the room where Mr. Shalloub stood helpless.

He heard the words "Allah ya samhak." May God forgive you. Then BANG. Then silence. Then BANG. Then a thump and the floor vibrated as though something heavy had just fallen. Then BANG. Abraham couldn't bear to look, couldn't bear to get up, could hardly bear to breathe.

# Chapter Six

Abraham couldn't remember raising himself from that cold floor, couldn't remember being treated for the head wound that he had received from Mr. Kalashnikov, couldn't remember returning home. But clearly he had done all these things. Or rather they had been done for him. He was in a state of shock, and it was clear that his days with the Red Cross had now come to their end.

In the next few weeks, it also became clear that there had been a ceasefire. The incessant sound of shooting and shelling had become more intermittent and finally almost nonexistent. About two weeks later Leyla came and told his mother that school was to start on Monday. His mother knocked on his door but he didn't want to face Leyla like this. He had been in bed most of the time and looked like something from a horror novel.

Abraham finally consented to leave his room the weekend before classes were to resume. Raymond had been especially insistent, finally getting entrance to his room.

"Mom probably sent you here," Abraham said, sitting on the corner of his bed.

"Your mom can be pretty convincing," Raymond allowed. "She's called me every day saying she can't get you out of this room."

"And she thinks you can?"

"Look Abraham. You did what you could. You did your best for Mr. Shalloub."

"Did I?" Abraham asked, but to no one in particular. "Have you spoken with Abdullah?"

"He's pretty much the same as you, staying in his room. I tried to talk to him but he didn't really want to. I don't think he knows you were there."

There was a long silence. Both men looked at the floor. Then Raymond brightened.

"Come on, let's have one last weekend together. You, Me, Leyla, Roger. I don't think Abdullah is up for it, but..."

"What do you mean 'one last?'" Abraham was finally drawn to consider something outside of his head for the first time in weeks.

"You know things will start up again," Raymond said, and then he looked down at the floor, trying to summon up words he knew his friend would not want to hear. "And when they do I feel I have to fight."

"You're joining the Christian militia," Abraham said with an air of resignation. It was a step he knew Raymond had been contemplating.

"I feel like I have to. We can't let them take over."

"Them?" Abraham was incredulous. "'They' are Mr. Shalloub. 'They' are Abdullah. 'They' are Leyla."

"Son, are you OK?" The voice came through the closed door and Abraham realized he had begun yelling.

"Yes, Mom. I'm OK."

They both waited until they heard her footsteps fade from the hallway.

"And none of them can be protected without a gun. Leyla and Abdullah and Mr. Shalloub mean nothing to the Muslim militia."

"And they mean something to the Christian militia?"

Raymond had no answer.

"Just go. I'll pick you up tomorrow at 5. Maybe getting you drunk will give you a little more good sense. Or maybe we will just break both your legs."

The next day Abraham picked up Roger and Raymond. The German shepherd, who now followed Abraham everywhere, was in the backseat. Leyla caught a ride to the club in the center of the city where they agreed to meet. It still wasn't safe for Abraham to come into the Muslim sector.

"Are you going to take this boy inside?" Leyla asked, stooping to give the dog a scratch on the ears.

"No, he'll wait for me out here," Abraham said. "He waits for me and follows me everywhere I go."

"Have you given him a name?"

"I've hardly noticed he's a 'him.'"

At that moment the first chords of "It Don't Come Easy," Ringo Starr's first big hit after the breakup of the Beatles, came wafting out of the pub.

"What about 'Ringo?'" Leyla immediately brightened.

"What? It's not even your dog!" Abraham retorted.

"Oh please," Leyla now held the dog's face close to hers and she poked her lip out in an expression of pouting. "It's perfect. Ringo Starr is my favorite musician in my favorite band. It will help me get over the breakup."

Leyla had taken the breakup of the Beatles hard. She had grown up with the band. Her mom played the White Album constantly and had worn out the needle on the record player. Abraham had bought the family a lightly used record player and earned the undying gratitude of Leyla's mom.

"OK, 'Ringo' it is. But don't be surprised if I just call him "Mutt.""

"He's no mutt," Leyla said, now looking directly into the dark brown canine eyes while the dog panted expectantly. "He's pure German shepherd I have no doubt. And by the way." She now rubbed her hands on both sides of his head, causing it to move back and forth with her words. "I'm a he."

"OK, boy, you wait out here."

Leyla and Abraham entered the pub and seated themselves next to Roger and Raymond, who had bypassed the dog talk, at the bar.

"You know the school has moved into the old school near the American embassy," Leyla said between sips of red wine. "The old school is pretty badly damaged."

"Yeah, I heard. I'll be there Monday," Abraham assured her.

"It's a nice old building with a little courtyard. Maybe we can hang out there."

"I'm not sure how much 'hanging out' we're going to be able to do." Abraham lit a cigarette.

"I thought you were going to try to stop," Leyla said while giving Abraham a friendly punch in the shoulder.

"If I live long enough to die of lung cancer, I'll have beaten the odds."

"That sounds like a reason for a toast," Roger said, standing and raising his beer. "Here's to dying of lung cancer."

The three others stood and clinked glasses and deep in Abraham's heart he felt a sense of despair, that this was the last moment of joyous rebellion they'd be allowed together before forces unseen drove them apart.

On Monday morning, Abraham walked into the new classroom in the old building that was being reopened to host the school. First he saw Ahmed with his familiar unironed shirt. Then he looked toward the class and was struck by who he didn't see. No Raymond and no Hussein. They were both preparing to fight on opposite sides, perhaps even to kill each other. Also missing, of course, was Abdullah. Who knew when, or if, he would recover from the loss of his father. That left 19 others, seven Muslims and 12 Christians aside from Abraham himself.

The next thing that occurred to Abraham was that no one seemed to notice his entrance. Everyone's eyes were transfixed on the front of the classroom, even though Ahmed was seated at his desk and clearly hadn't begun class. Everyone's eyes, except those of the fanatics. Most of them were talking, laughing. Marwan especially had a smug look of superiority.

As Abraham neared the desks he turned on his heels and swung his head toward the front of the class. What he saw made him stumble into his seat, spilling his books. This broke the hypnosis that the other 19o students had come under and they turned their attention to the noise of Abraham clumsily finding his place.

But now Abraham's attention was transfixed on the chalkboard. On that board, is neat Arabic script, were written the words:

"In this classroom there are 7 heroes and 13 pigs."

"Would anyone like to explain this?" Ahmed said, raising himself from his desk. "Anyone?"

"Whoever did this, I want you to come up here right now and erase it. Otherwise, believe me, I can find a way to make you all pay."

At that Abraham stood from his seat. It was a move that clearly stunned even Ahmed who rarely was rattled.

"Mr. Hajjar, what are you doing?" he asked.

"Abraham, it couldn't be," Leyla was clearly confused and her voice trailed off.

"I'm taking responsibility." Abraham said, with a confidence that neither Leyla nor Ahmed nor anyone else in that classroom had ever seen in him.

He strode purposefully to the front of the classroom, picked up the eraser and removed the offending sentence from the board. He started to walk back to his seat but something occurred to him and you could see an almost imperceptible smile raise the corners of his lips and narrow his eyes. He turned back to the board, took the chalk and wrote in the place of the erasure:

"In this classroom there are 19 heroes and 1 coward."

Abraham turned back toward the class.

"Any questions?"

"I have one," Marwan now stood beside his desk. "Why only one coward?"

"Only one person wrote that on the chalkboard," Abraham replied without missing a beat. "God knows who that one person is. But, whoever he is, he is evidently too cowardly to admit it before us."

The smile drained from Marwan's face and he sat slowly back into his chair.

For the first time in his life, a life filled with childish whims and personal failures, of frightened recalcitrance and general impotence, Abraham felt like a man. He knew his place, and he returned to his seat. Leyla smiled softly. Abraham felt within himself that he had finally done something worthy of earning her respect.

# Chapter Seven

The next day was among the happiest of Abraham's life, in retrospect, the last hopeful day of his life. He could imagine the war might not restart, that he would graduate and lead a normal life in Beirut, much like his father had.

The following Wednesday all of that started to change. Abraham had never arrived at class without being greeted by the rumpled shirt of Ahmed, glasses down to the bridge of his nose, reviewing the lesson for the day. But on Wednesday his chair was empty.

Abraham took his seat in front of Leyla.

"What's up?" he asked in tone halfway between worry and nonchalance.

"Roger went by Ahmed's house," she said in a low tone, though the class was quiet enough that most could likely hear what she was saying. "The door to his flat was open and Ahmed was nowhere to be seen. But nothing seemed to be messed up. Very strange."

"Does Ahmed not have a family?"

"Not as far as I can tell. We asked the university president and he said he believed he has a father and that he would try to contact him."

After a couple of moments Abraham realized that a normally menacing presence was gone.

"Have you seen Marwan?" Abraham asked.

"No. I got here before anyone. I wanted to get some lab work done with the new computer setup and I've seen everyone come and go. No Marwan."

Abraham turned his head fully around and met Leyla's eyes. They were deep brown and the irises were large and looked into Abraham with a deep seriousness.

"Abraham, I'm starting to get a little nervous."

"I know." Abraham knew that their newly acquired computer skills were highly sought after in the new world of computer-aided warfare. And even if your side couldn't recruit you, the opposing side was likely to take you out to keep you from being recruited.

At that moment Joseph, the woman-hating professor, walked in the door.

"OK, class. It seems something has detained Ahmed. You may go home today. Hopefully everything will be back to normal tomorrow."

Things were not back to normal the next day. Joseph asked the class to bring him up to date on what their curriculum had been so he could hastily devise a backup plan. Twenty-four hours had passed and Ahmed was still missing. For that matter so was Marwan.

That day Abraham had lunch with Roger, Raymond and Leyla in the courtyard of their new, old school complex. They quietly chewed their sandwiches, trying hard not to contemplate what could have happened to Ahmed. Leyla leisurely snapped off pieces of her sandwich to share with Ringo who was lounging with the group.

"You know," said Leyla. "I had hoped this small garden could become our oasis. But now I know that cannot be. There will be no more refuges for us in this city."

"Is your family going to try to get out?" Roger asked.

"I don't think so. All they ever talk about is going home."

"Home" for Leyla's parents, Abraham knew, was a country that no longer existed, Palestine. It was now Israel and there seemed little chance that Palestinians could ever go back.

"But," she said, "it is not my home. I've never been to Palestine. I'm a woman without a country." Her face then brightened. "I plan on going to Paris. I have a cousin there. It's a different world. When I go we can all meet up and walk the Champs Elysees."

Only briefly Abraham's mind wandered back to the French girl, still his sole sexual encounter. He wondered where she was. Many of the French families had returned to France when war broke out. Europeans couldn't imagine living in a place as dangerous as Lebanon, especially those young enough to have no memory of World War II.

"Do you think it was a mistake?" Abraham asked.

"Do I think what was a mistake?" Leyla responded.

"Writing what I did on the board. Was I just needlessly stirring them up?"

"Never ask that question again," Leyla looked straight ahead at no one in particular. She had that determination in her voice that Abraham was accustomed to, but still could be startled by. "When we bow to cowards like Marwan we become something less than human ourselves. I don't want to live if it means licking the feet of tyrants like that."

"OK," Abraham leaned back on his elbows and looked toward the sky. "I promise. I won't ask that question again."

That evening Abraham slept soundly. The cease fire continued, but Abraham sensed a bit of a cease fire in his heart. He was at peace with his decisions and, whatever the future held, he was confident that he could always lean on the intense determination of the woman who had now become his best friend, his confidant, his rock in a world that seemed to be changing by the day.

The next morning was a beautiful, sunny day. Abraham's mother had made kibbeh, a sort of croquet stuffed with lamb that he knew Leyla especially loved. He packed a half dozen extra for their lunch in the courtyard, and he thought about the relish with which she would savor each and every one.

When he arrived at school he was puzzled to find a hastily written note attached to the door: "Class canceled today." He heard voices that were coming from the courtyard where he and Leyla and Roger and Raymond regularly ate their lunch. He could tell there was a larger crowd hovering over something in the middle of the courtyard, almost exactly in the area where the four often ate. Rocky, who had followed him to school as he always did, started whimpering.

"What happened?" Abraham asked one of the students standing near the entrance to the courtyard, farthest from the mass of humanity at the center.

"They found a body this morning. Looks like someone was murdered," the student answered.

Immediately Abraham's thoughts went to Ahmed Musawi, the instructor with the eternally crinkled shirt and eyeglasses on the bridge of his nose. He had been missing now for a couple of days and he had no doubt that Marwan had it out for him. His heart sank at the thought of it.

"It's Mr. Musawi isn't it?" Abraham offered.

"No. I'm pretty sure it's a girl. And I think I heard someone say it was a student."

Abraham felt as though he had been struck by lightning. A shock surged through his body. Slowly he started to push his way through the students toward the mass of humanity in the middle. He was not the most religious of students, but he started saying within himself, "Dear God, please, no, please. Make it someone else."

As he came within a few yards of the group he saw something off to his left. It was the green purse, the one that was perhaps Leyla's only prized possessions. He went toward it and picked it up, hoping somehow to identify it as a different green purse. He picked it up and felt

42

with the tips of the fingers of his right hand the "Hermes" name plate attached to the front. He dropped the bag to the ground and turned slowly toward the group huddled around the body. Finally he gathered the strength to hurl himself into the group. He wedged himself between the hips of two male students.

There before him was the sight that would stick with him until the day he died. He would see it every time he closed his eyes, every time he tried to sleep. When sleep would come he would see it in his dreams, his nightmares. Leyla's face, drained of its determination, its calm independence, her eyes half opened, half closed, a wide gash in her neck but no blood underneath. Her hair matted with dried blood. She had clearly been brought here from somewhere else. Her clothes were disheveled, her blouse ripped, her jacket now laid over her in a frail attempt at preserving dignity.

Abraham dropped to his knees. He wanted to scream or to cry or to show some sort of animal response to what he saw before him but nothing came out. He felt empty in his core.

At first all sound became silent as he stared at Leyla's lifeless face, but finally he started to hear voices, one of them especially insistent, that seemed to be addressing the crowd.

"Where are the police? They don't care about a Palestinian girl. They're not going to look for the perpetrator who raped our Muslim sister. We have to find him ourselves."

Abraham recognized the voice. It was one of the fanatics who was in the club when Marwan had called Leyla a whore.

"You know very well who did this."

"Yes I do. No doubt one of your Christian militia friends. Probably Raymond. Maybe Leyla was the easiest Muslim victim he could find."

Abraham swung as hard as he could and felt the fanatic's face crackle in the midst of his fist.

The fanatic crumpled to the ground and Abraham pounced on top of him.

"You know that asshole Marwan did this," Abraham screamed as loud as his lungs would allow. He started flailing his fists into the crumpled mass of fanatic on the ground when suddenly he was seized on either side by arms much stronger than his. He realized that all those standing around the body had been friends of the fanatics. The rape and killing of a Palestinian girl could be the spark that lit the fuse of the bomb that was Beirut in 1976. He felt their fists striking his body.

He was happy. They would, if he was fortunate, kill him right here. He would join Leyla. That was an outcome greatly to be desired. But suddenly the fists stopped. He was pulled away from the crowd by a violent force. When he looked around, through the sweat and blood dripping down his face that he was being dragged away from the crowd by guards from his father's bank.

He heard a pop.

"Someone's got a gun," one of the guards told the other. "Let's get out of here."

A car was idling by the front of the school. The guards pushed him into the back.

"Ringo!" he yelled. "Don't leave Ringo."

One Elias' associates opened the back door and when Ringo saw Abraham in the backseat, he immediately hopped in.

When Abraham looked up, he saw his father's face turned toward him from the passenger side of the front seat.

"Father! How did you know to come?"

"I heard that a Palestinian girl had been killed at the university. I knew it could be a tricky situation, but I didn't know you would be in the middle of it. Did you know her well?"

"Yes father," Abraham responded, his eyes downcast.

"Well, that's too bad. I imagine school will be closed for awhile. If you'd like you may come with me to the bank."

"Take me home."

Abraham spent the next week in his room. He hardly ate. His mother came up with a tray of food three times a day. Three times a day he refused it. Every day she would peek into the room and every day she would see him staring off into nothingness.

After three days she considered some sort of force feeding.

"Abraham, you must eat something," she said from behind the door to his bedroom.

"I'm not hungry."

She opened the door, "Abraham this is ridiculous. Are you going to mope for the rest of your life?"

"What's ridiculous is this world. This city. These groups that kill each other. For what?"

Abraham's mother sat gingerly at the edge of his bed. "I don't know. I do know that people have been killing each other longer than you or I have been alive. And they will be killing each other after we are dead."

She took a kibbeh ball and placed it into his hand.

"You know," he said, eyeing the ball of fried lamb's meat intently, "I had packed some of these the day Leyla died. She really loved your kibbeh, Mom." He began to sob.

Abraham's mother drew her son toward her bosom.

"I'm sorry, my son. I didn't know you had such a friendship with a Palestinian girl."

He drew his head back from her chest.

"Is that the only way you can think of her? A Palestinian girl?" he smiled, and chuckled with a hollow laughter. "If I were half the human being she was, I think I would be someone of whom you could be proud."

She held out another kibbeh and pressed it into his mouth.

"She was Palestinian. I do not know what that is like, but she was a woman in Lebanon. I do know what that is like. I know it is not always easy. She was a woman pursuing a university education. I can only imagine what that is like."

He chewed the lamb's meat slowly.

"I am proud of you, my son. Not only that you are smart and sensitive, but that you are wise enough not to be intimidated by a woman who is your equal. I have spent my life pretending to not know, not understand, letting the men around me explain things I already knew so that they could feel their superiority. Your friend did not do that. I am afraid that may be why she died. I'm sorry I was too occupied with my life to get to know your friend. But I do know this. If she was who you say she was, she would tell you to get out of this room and do something."

Abraham swallowed the kibbeh. "What am I supposed to do?" His eyes were swollen and bloodshot.

His mother took his face in her hands the way she had when he was 5. With her thumb she wiped a lone tear from his cheek.

"You must fight."

# Chapter Eight

It could be argued that the murder of Leyla Jarred was in its own way a seminal moment in the Lebanese civil war, in the same way the wind created from the flutter of a butterfly's wing can stir the atmosphere and spawn a hurricane. Hurricanes would happen anyway, it just so happened that this particular flutter started a chain of events that caused the on-again, off-again conflict to become on-again.

At first the conflict was among the classmates. Those who were in the computer science department knew well that the perpetrator of this murder likely was Marwan and definitely was someone from among the fanatics. The Palestinian students began arguing with the students known to have sided with the fanatics. This led to fist fights. Hours had passed and no police came to investigate the killing. When authorities did arrive they were not police but soldiers from the rapidly disintegrating Lebanese Army. Their interest was in clearing the school, not in investigating a murder.

Leyla's parents were cradling their daughter's body, now wrapped in a white sheet one of the Palestinian students had retrieved. Finally, around nightfall, a stretcher from the Red Cross was procured and Leyla's body was taken back to her parents in the Palestinian camp where she had lived.

Westerners may have a difficult time distinguishing one Middle Eastern Muslim group from the next, but the inhabitants of the region have no such difficulty. When Palestinians lost their homeland in1948, they began a migration to neighboring countries, notably Jordan and Lebanon. Those fortunate enough to make it to the relatively rural nation of Jordan were eventually assimilated into the populace and soon became the majority. In Lebanon, a land already rent by multiple religious and ethnic loyalties, the Palestinians were quickly isolated in multiple camps run by the United Nations.

Over time tents were replaced with semi-permanent structures and even some factories benefited from the cheap labor the Palestinians offered.

They were cheap because they were and are barred by law from most professions. In Lebanon there are no Palestinian doctors or lawyers, no Palestinian engineers or bankers. In fact, until 2005, there weren't even any Palestinian secretaries. What Palestinians such as Leyla could do is go to school. This was not so much to educate the population on the part of the Lebanese government, as it was an effort to make the Palestinians attractive enough workers that some other country might take a few of them out of Lebanon.

This was the slum to which Leyla's body was returned by her grieving parents. Over the next several days the local population erupted in protests and riots. These climaxed on the day of Leyla's funeral, during which her shrouded body was carried throughout the neighborhood. The Christian militias which held sway over the area kept a tenuous watch over the proceedings. But finally the inevitable happened. Someone among the rioting crowd shot at the Christian militia soldiers, prompting a swift response.

Homes were burned. Inhabitants were in many cases summarily shot, including Leyla's own parents. Leyla's body, it can only be presumed, was hastily buried — somewhere.

The day after the massacre, Abdullah showed up at the Hajjar home. Abraham's mother quickly ushered him inside. It was quite dangerous for a Muslim to be found in a Christian neighborhood. She brought him to Abraham's door.

This was the first time Abraham had seen Abdullah since his father's death. They sat in silence for some minutes before Abdullah finally said. "It's over. It's all over."

Abraham said nothing in response to this. He merely looked up into Abdullah's eyes, now welling with tears.

"It wasn't a bad dream, you know," Abdullah continued. "You and me and Leyla and Roger. That we could get real jobs, have real families, have a real life. But it's ... that's ... that's gone."

"Have you heard anything about why she was taken?" Abraham asked tentatively.

"I've asked around. Some said they heard her calling Marwan a pig and that they had no doubt he did this to her."

"I should have seen the danger. I should have done something."

"What could you have done? Go to the funeral? You wouldn't have lasted an hour there. Abraham," at this he placed his hands on Abraham's shoulders and turned Abraham's body towards his. "This is not your fault. It is Marwan's."

After this, a pause, and then Abdullah continued. "I wanted to let you know I am joining the brigades."

"NO! Abdullah you are a geek. You say I wouldn't last an hour in the midst of a Palestinian camp. How can you survive as a soldier?"

"I don't know, but I have to. For my father. For Leyla. I have to do something."

Now he placed his hands on Abraham's shoulders again. "And I promise you. I will find Marwan. And I will kill him."

Though Abraham wanted to protest this insane idea, he was glad, glad that there was a real man like Abdullah who could avenge Leyla's death, someone much better than he. What was he? How would Abraham describe himself? A coward? If he had been among the fanatics no doubt they would call him a sissy, a woman. But that could not be so. Leyla was a woman, but she had been exponentially more bold, more powerful than he could ever be. She had the traits he despised himself for lacking.

"Yes," said Abraham forcefully. "You will kill Marwan. Please do it before you get yourself killed."

After Abdullah left, Abraham felt better. He began to eat, to breathe, to walk about despite the danger of shelling as the belligerents began their battles.

Elias and Maya were especially pleased to see Abraham come out of his room. Their only child had seemed unreachably depressed, really, since the killing of old Mr. Shalloub, no, actually before that, since the beginning of school. Maya worried about her son incessantly, Elias not so much so. He held the masculine attitude that this was just a phase of adolescent boyhood, that his son would one day snap out of his funk and become ready to face the world, whatever that means. Maya was working on some of the alterations she was taking in from their neighbor, the Armenian couple Arthur and Ani Zakaryan.

One morning, after having just such a conversation, Elias bid his wife goodbye and he started off toward his bank in his car, a drive of just a couple of kilometers. Despite the short distance, Maya wished her husband would use the car and driver made available by his bank. Beirut had simply become too dangerous a place to drive around alone, especially for a banker.

But Elias was a stubborn old man, and he was undeniably becoming an old man, both in attitude and manner.

As he drove down the street he passed daily to the bank, he noticed something he had not seen on this route before, but of which he had heard. As various brigades made their claims to control of various

48

neighborhoods, they would set up checkpoints. Their purpose was to make their presence known and to exert their authority. They were called *hajez tayar*, or "flying checkpoints." This one was manned only by two men standing next to what looked to be a portable booth, hardly larger than a phone booth.

"Excuse me, sir, let me see your identification," the man, who sported a rifle slung across his chest, said to Elias. Elias dutifully produced the documents. The man turned away and spoke into his portable radio. Soon a dark sedan came out of a nearby alleyway.

"Mr. Hajjar, please exit your vehicle."

His first instinct was to hit the gas and run, but he knew he would surely be cut down. If he was shot down there would be no investigation, no trial, no consequence. Beirut was now a lawless place and what law you could garner came from which brigade or gang with which you had good connections. He knew getting out of his car and into the dark sedan was almost certain death, but refusing was absolutely certain death, so he took the only action that was reasonable at this point. He got out of the car. As he started to get into the dark sedan the soldier stopped him.

"Hold on. I need your keys."

The soldier gave a slight chuckle and reached into his pocket to retrieve the key. He then pushed Elias with force the rest of the way into the back seat and slammed the door.

"What do you want?" he asked as the driver, whose face he never saw, sped them through the streets westward toward the Muslim sector.

"You will find out soon enough," came the only reply he would get until they reached their destination.

He now realized that there was a man seated in the passenger side, who turned around and produced a sort of cloth bag, which was placed over Elias' head. He now had a bit of hope, because he knew that they cared about him not knowing the route to his place of confinement, an that meant they had an intention of releasing him alive.

After a drive of about 45 minutes, the car entered a place of darkness, as the little light that had shown through the weave of his mask was now extinguished and the sound of the motor reverberated off the walls. After about 12 turns to the right, the car came to a stop, his door was opened and he was pulled out by his left arm. Surely his captor realized how frail the old man now was by the way that bony arm must have felt in his muscular hand.

He was half-dragged, half-led for about 50 paces before he was stopped and he could hear his captor knocking on a door. The door opened and he was led inside and into an interior room in whatever apartment or office he had been led into. It smelled of sweat and mold and of spices like sumac and curry.

The door to his room was closed and he could tell he was alone now and he could barely make out the words being used by the men in the next room who were no doubt reporting their catch.

He could hear the words "banker" and "ransom" and "Samir will be pleased."

When the door once again opened he could hear the faint ringing that a telephone makes when it is being moved and ringing mechanism is being jostled. The phone was slammed on a table that was in front of him.

Finally his head cover was removed and, since he had already been in the dark, his eyes immediately adjusted to the dark room. He saw the faces of five men, but he almost let out a small cry when he saw the one in the middle. The "Samir" who would be pleased was none other than the security guard of his bank, the man who almost a year ago he had gone to with the promise of a surgery to cure an almost paralyzing back condition, a surgery that, it seemed now unfortunate to Elias, had evidently worked quite well.

He felt a pulse of anger, of betrayal. He imagined that Samir had joined this group, whatever it was, and had betrayed Elias to them as someone for whom the bank would produce a hefty ransom. But, of course, he was quite unsure that the bank would indeed produce a dime for him. The bank was suffering greatly with the flight of those with means out of the country. And even if it did have the means to pay the ransom, he was not at all sure that he was that valuable to the bank. Indeed, his primary area of expertise, which was domestic investments, was increasingly unnecessary. There wasn't a lot of capital investment going on in Beirut these days.

But his anger was checked when he realized that the look he saw on the face of Samir was one of shock followed by dejection and disappointment.

"We must release him," Samir stated firmly, a statement that brought a shocked expression to the faces of the other four.

"What are you talking about? This is a vice president of the Bank of Paris?"

"You don't know what you're talking about. I'm the one who worked there." He now looked straight at Elias. "He was nothing more than an office manager, overseeing the secretaries."

Elias realized that it was the course of wisdom not to say anything. The other four hustled Samir out of the room and shut the door behind them. He heard more excited talking in what he now recognized as a hallway outside his door. This did indeed seem to be some sort of apartment and, as far as he could tell, neither Samir nor any of his compatriots were soldier or associated with any of the known brigades. He guessed that they had merely formed an opportunistic gang and were aiming at making money through hostage-taking and extortion.

He had no more contact, except to be given a tepid cup of foul water, for the rest of the evening. But late that night he was awakened by Samir, who placed before him a cold cup of clear water and a fresh piece of flatbread.

"Hello, boss," Samir whispered. "Sorry we must meet under such unfortunate circumstances."

"What are you doing here?" Elias asked.

"Well, I couldn't work as a security guard, and there are few options for a man like me, old and washed up. But I do know security. I know how to convince people you are an authority. So this group, they are looking out for the people who are losing the most in this war. I joined them hoping to help those who have no means of support. But in many ways they are no more than common thieves. Please forgive me."

"What are they going to do?"

"I have a plan. I've tried to convince them that you are not worth it to the bank to pay."

"I'm not," Elias interrupted.

"Perhaps," Samir said. "But you don't know. I have someone on the inside of the bank who will string them along until we can find the opportunity to get you out of here."

"Who do you have inside the bank?"

"Elias. You know I can't tell you."

"I know," Elias paused for a moment. "You know Samir. In the old Beirut, people like me held all the cards. We had the power. Now," and Elias' eyes fixed themselves on the gun holstered on Samir's belt, "the only power in Beirut is the gun."

"I know *sadiqi*," Samir said while grasping his shoulder, "My friend. You were kind to me when you held the power. I will do my best to be kind to you while I hold the gun."

The next morning one of the four thugs came back into the room with a phone. He dialed a number on a piece of paper.

"Hello," came the answer through the speaker of the receiver.

"Hello," the thug said into the mouthpiece. "Am I speaking to Ziad Ismail, president of the Bank of Paris?"

"This is he."

"I represent a group that has come into possession of a friend of yours. Perhaps you would like to speak to him."

The man then handed the receiver to Elias. He had never heard the name Ziad Ismail in his life.

"Hello Ziad, old friend. I want you to know I am quite well. My hosts have not mistreated me."

The voice on the other end feigned surprise, and Elias did his best job of trying to comfort him.

"It is OK. Just do as they ask."

The thug then took the receiver back.

"We will need 500,000 pounds for his return."

Before the war started, three Lebanese pounds would get you a U.S. dollar. At this point, it was five pounds to the dollar. by the end of the war it would be 1,500.

"I will need time."

"You have 48 hours."

The thug slammed the phone down. He turned to Elias.

"We will see how valuable an employee you are."

His only meals were cold kishek, a sort of porridge made with bulgur wheat, but from time to time Samir would smuggle him some bread. As the hours passed he could tell the patience of the four thugs was growing thin. They made several more calls to the dummy phone number. Samir's stooge on the other side had stopped answering the calls.

On the second day after his kidnapping, the four thugs and Samir came back into the room. Samir looked as though he had been in a fight.

The thug who had made the phone call again tapped the phone and said, "Your bank doesn't seem to think you are a valuable employee. I think it is time you called your wife."

"No," Samir interjected. "His wife could barely give us a thousand pounds. I told you he is a low-level employee."

"Is that so? He had a pretty nice car."

"Then keep the car. It's the most valuable thing we'll get out of him."

"What about trying the wife? Maybe she'd could come up with a little more if we got her on the phone and let her know the kind of ordeal her husband was going through."

At that, the thug turned suddenly and struck the old man bound to the chair in the abdomen. The air in his lungs raced out, causing a high-pitched shriek.

"Or maybe we should just be done with him."

The thug took his gun and placed it against Elias' head. He could feel the round, cold barrel at his temple. He knew each moment could be his last. He became aware of the slow passage of time, of his heart beating, the tears at the corners of his eyes clinched shut. He uttered silent prayers within himself. Dear God, if only you let me live, let me see Maya and Abraham just once more. Then he heard a click. Though his eyes were closed he could only see white. Then he became aware that his heart was still beating, the tears were still on his cheek, time was still passing. The gun was without a bullet. He opened his eyes and could see the thug grab the head covering. He gruffly stuffed Elias' head into it. He told Samir to take him away.

The knock on the door of the Hajjar home in Broumana was answered first by Ringo's excited barking and then by a woman with red, swollen eyes who clearly hadn't slept well for days. It took Elias a moment to see in those eyes the familiar spark he had always associated with Maya. Once Maya recognized it was indeed Elias she flung the door open and embraced him. Immediately she realized he might not yet be safe. She jerked back from the embrace and looked into the street.

"Are you alone?" she asked.

"Yes my dear. And I apologize that I no longer have my car. I believe it is the price of my freedom."

Abraham had heard the commotion downstairs and momentarily forgot to be despondent. He came running down the stairs.

"*Abi*, where were you? We were worried sick!" he exclaimed as he embraced his father.

"It is," said Elias, "a long story."

It is a story that in many ways he refused to tell his wife and son. He would downplay the danger he faced, saying merely that some confused partisans had captured him and that when they realized they had the wrong fellow they released him. But there was no denying that the man they released was different than the man they had captured.

He now would not go anywhere without the man his bank provided to serve the dual purpose of driver and bodyguard. He rarely went out at night and when he did it was only for short distances for a very specific purpose. And one of those purposes was increasingly to attend church. Elias Hajjar, a man who had to this point only nominally been Christian began attending Mass each morning and was volunteering to serve various lay functions at the nearby church.

Elias had a good friend, Charbel, who was the driver for the archbishop. Charbel felt indebted to Elias because he had been given a second job at the bank to make ends meet, a driver's pay not being enough to feed four hungry kids. To show his gratitude, Charbel had taught Maya and later Abraham how to drive using the archbishop's very own car. Charbel was able to suggest to the archbishop that Elias be put on the lay board overseeing the relief work in the parish.

One morning Abraham decided to accompany his father to Mass to observe, and perhaps to understand, this newfound reverence. Abraham himself had always longed to find some sort of spiritual fulfillment, but he had plainly seen that while religion seemed to make some good people better, it made bad people worse, regardless of what kind of religion they practiced.

While listening to the liturgy and facing the father and the crucifix, Abraham asked what had prompted such piety.

"I know many pious people who have died in this war," Elias told Abraham while his gaze was still transfixed on the large golden crucifix at the altar. "I know many prayers to live have gone unanswered, and I don't know why God didn't answer their prayers. But I know that he answered mine, and for that reason I must keep my promise and come every week to kneel before him."

# Chapter Nine

In the aftermath of these two traumatic events, Leyla's murder and Elias' kidnapping, the Hajjar family was irreversibly changed. Lebanon, home to their ancestors for centuries, perhaps millennia, now felt like an alien wasteland, threatening, hostile. The lines of battle were drawing ominously close to their Broumana home. Elias' church work, while satisfying, was not giving him the peace of mind that he had hoped it would. He was beginning to consider what was once unthinkable.

To leave Lebanon would be to start all over. Though Beirut was a mess, its institutions continued — the bank, the church, the community. Elias had a place in all of these and if he fled he would have no place at all, a daunting prospect at the age of 50.

But he would not be completely without a foothold to climb the mountain of a new life.

Maya had a younger brother Michael who had been living in the U.S. for over a decade. After graduating from the American University of Beirut in pharmacology he took a job with a pharmaceutical company in Boston and had lived there ever since. Michael and Maya were very close because their parents had died when Michael was 16 and Maya 22. Elias and Maya had taken Michael in while he finished school and Elias had looked after him and had filled in the financial gap that Michael and Maya's parents' premature death had left in his college fund.

Before the troubles began, Michael would call Elias and Maya, telling them with relish of the things that pleased him about the U.S. — the wide open spaces he encountered when he got outside the big cities, even the way that drivers would scrupulously stop at red lights even in the middle of the night with little to no traffic. He had asked Elias and Maya to pay him a visit and contemplate moving, but Elias would have none of it — until now.

Like a doctor who had decided all possible cures had been tried and nothing was left but to let the patient die, Elias knew there was nothing left for him in Lebanon and there was little hope that would change in his lifetime.

Elias called Michael and asked about coming to stay for a month on a tourist visa and hiring an immigration attorney — the attorney being another thing Michael said America was famous for — and investigating the possibility of asylum or perhaps being sponsored by a potential employer.

It was decided that Abraham and Maya would stay in a flat adjacent to Charbel's. The archbishop's driver and the man for whom Elias and once been patron, now found himself in the position of paying back the favor.

Had this war happened 20 years previous, Charbel would no doubt have been the one fleeing Lebanon, but now, a man in his 60s but who seemed closer to his 80s, could not start over. So, he decided, he would lend a helping hand to a family who could.

He had a full head of gray hair and a gray mustache and kind, blue eyes. He was benevolent with Abraham because he knew he'd been through much. He could tell the toll that the war had taken on him without knowing the specifics of Leyla's death. He had allowed Abraham to bring Ringo into the flat even though, as property of diocese, dogs technically were not allowed. But he could tell that this new addition to the family was important to Abraham.

The Hajjars took advantage of a lull in the fighting to get Elias on a plane bound for Boston by way of Geneva. At the airport Elias, a man who tended to have little physical contact with his family, embraced his son with a solid hug.

"You are the man for awhile," Elias said in his son's ear. "You take care of your mom for me."

He then embraced his wife and turned on his heels to face the gate at the Beirut airport.

"I am going to a new world," Elias said, half to himself and half to his family. "I wonder how I will do."

He then began taking decisive steps until he had walked outside the doors leading to the steps of the airplane. Abraham embraced his mother until the saw him step inside.

Elias would never step foot on Lebanese soil again.

"He'll be alright, Mom," Abraham said softly. "We'll see him soon."

"I hope so," Maya replied. Then turned toward Charbel.

"I don't know how to thank you for all you're doing for us."

"I could never turn my back on the family of my friend," Charbel replied. He tossed his keys to Abraham, who caught them out of the air.

"I'm taking the afternoon off. You drive us home Abraham."

Over the next month, conditions in Beirut deteriorated quickly.

Twice the windows of their flat shattered when bombs detonated near the church compound. Once when walking to the store with Ringo, Abraham crossed paths with the archbishop, who was out for his morning walk. As they passed, the archbishop bid Abraham a good morning and Ringo jumped up on the archbishop, giving him a slobbery greeting.

"Get off him," Abraham chided as he pulled his now large dog from the cleric. He could see the disgust on the father's face.

"Very sorry," Abraham offered. At that moment Ringo's ears perked up and he took off running into the entrance of the rectory. Instinctively Abraham and the archbishop followed. Moments later a shell exploded on the very spot where just a few seconds previously Ringo had slobbered on the archbishop.

The blast knocked the archbishop off his feet.

"Are you OK father?" Abraham asked as he helped the ecclesiastic up.

"Oh my son. I should learn to appreciate dogs. I've never been fond of them, but yours just saved our lives."

He gave Ringo and appreciative scratch to the ears and looked around the rectory to his secretary. "Everyone OK?"

"I think so," the secretary replied. "Just startled. When will all of this end?"

"It doesn't seem it ever will." The archbishop then turned to Abraham. "I think it may soon be time for you to join your father."

A couple of days later, the archbishop and Charbel stopped by the flat with a plan for getting Maya and Abraham out of Beirut, but first they needed to know if Elias was coming back.

"Things seem to be going well," Maya said as she handed the archbishop a cup of tea. "Michael found an immigration attorney who is working on legal status and, here's the providential part, do you remember John Saleeba?"

"Very clearly," the archbishop said before taking a slurp of the hot liquid. "He was the manager of one of the branches of your husband's bank. His family left, what is it? Seven years ago?"

"Well, Elias was opening a local bank account at the Bank of Boston for the money we are able to send out of Lebanon. It just so happened that John walked by as Elias was doing this. John said that he thought there would be a place for him there and, given his banking knowledge, he might even convince the other officers to approve sponsoring him in the U.S. on a work-related visa."

"That does seem providential," the archbishop acknowledged.

"I think that might not be the only piece of providence," Charbel said. "The archbishop is scheduled to visit Paris next week and has already booked tickets. I will be driving him to the airport. The fighting is getting close to the airport and both sides want to control it. I have no idea how much longer it will remain open. If you don't go now, you might never be able to get out."

Maya knew this moment was inevitable. Though she had no desire to leave Lebanon, she also didn't want her son to have to live in a war zone, and definitely didn't want him to feel compelled to fight.

"What do you think Abraham. Are you ready?" she asked.

Abraham looked down at Ringo, who was lying on the floor having given up on the possibilities of making friends with the archbishop. "Can we take him?" he asked hesitantly.

"I have a large dog carrier," Charbel offered. "Don't ask me why I kept it, but we used to have a hunting dog for the former archbishop. The only bad thing is that the airline only gives you two pieces of checked luggage, so the dog would count as one of them."

"That's okay," Maya said. "We still have properties here in Beirut. When things calm down we'll need to come back anyway. We'll get the rest of our possessions then.

"Okay, then, let's do it." Abraham was not sad about leaving Lebanon. Most importantly, he hoped to somehow be reborn, because he knew that a large part of him had died with Leyla.

The following week Abraham and Charbel carried the dog cage and put it in the back of the van and shut the rear door. The diplomatic plates on the back of the van would afford them safe passage through most neighborhoods. Abraham and Maya then entered the van in the back seat. Charbel, of course, was driving. The archbishop sat in the front passenger seat.

"This looks like a very nice day for a getaway," he said. peering up into the partly cloudy sky through the front windshield.

As they drove the streets toward the airport, the sound of shelling got consistently louder as they neared the airport.

When they finally arrived, Charbel and Abraham pulled the dog from the back. The archbishop even helped. The SwissAir skycap took one look at the cage and said "You've got to be kidding me. Bombs are falling from the sky and you want us to fly your dog out of here?"

Abraham pulled out a $50 and pressed it into the man's hand. "Can you help us out here?" He looked hopefully into the skycap's face.

"This is the luckiest dog in Beirut," he said as he turned to place the tag on the crate. "I'm guessing you're going to Geneva as that's the only flight out today. Where are you headed after that?"

"Boston."

"I hope you're as lucky as this dog."

They left Ringo in the care of the skycap and headed into the terminal. It was a madhouse of foreigners trying to get out of Beirut before the airport closed, intermixed with Syrian soldiers who for now kept some semblance of peace in the main link between Lebanon and the outside world.

They headed through layer after layer of security. At each checkpoint, a soldier asked to see their visas. Being in the company of the archbishop seemed to help. He would be on the same plane to Geneva, before making his own connection to Paris.

Finally they made it onto the SwissAir flight. They could hear gunfire nearer and nearer the tarmac. Finally the stewardess shut the cabin door and Abraham turned to Maya. "That means we're actually getting out of here."

But 10 minutes later the stewardess took a phone call near the front of the plane and looked dejected. She opened the cabin door. At that moment the pilot came out of the cockpit.

"What are you doing?" the pilot asked the stewardess with a look of incredulity.

"You said the ATC tower has been hit. We cannot leave without ATC."

"Shut the door. We cannot stay."

The 300 or so passengers burst out in applause. But it was interrupted when one of the passengers said, "Oh my God. Look over there."

Passengers on the left side rushed over to look out the right side windows. What they saw was a military vehicle that was fighting to take control of the airport.

"Everybody back in their seats. Fasten your seat belt."

Before anyone could get to their seats, they felt the plane lurch forward. Abraham looked back at the military vehicle and could see militia waving machine guns and shooting in the air, trying to get the pilot's attention. They tried to keep up with the accelerating plane but fell behind as the plane reached takeoff velocity. The nose of the plane got off the ground and within seconds, Abraham could tell they were completely airborne.

He sat back in his seat and closed his eyes. He could see the plane as it must look from the now-vacant balcony of their Broumana home, as planes looked on those countless afternoons when he watched planes take off from the airport and he daydreamed about being aboard and going to distant places. He was now one of those on board, and he felt sorry for any young boys who were watching this plane taking off. It would be the last one for many months to come. They were now consigned to the hell that Beirut had become. And Abraham was being liberated.

# Chapter Ten

Abraham anticipated a quiet time exploring the international section of the Geneva airport. He had heard good things about the Swiss, that they were tolerant of foreigners, that they made outstanding chocolate. He thought about how good a strong coffee and a dark chocolate might taste in one of the shops while waiting for his flight to Boston. He was in for a rude awakening.

Immediately upon exiting the plane they were greeted on the ground by security officers.

"Get out your passports," barked a red-headed officer. "Those holding Lebanese passports to my left. Non-Lebanese to my right."

About two-thirds of the group, including Abraham and Maya, made their way to the left of the officer.

He led them into the airport and, once inside, immediately stopped in front of a door marked "security only."

"Who here has a connecting flight to the U.S.'" snapped the redhead. About half of the Lebanese, Abraham and his mother included, raised their hands.

"You who raised your hands come in here. The rest can go on to their next flight."

Abraham looked at his mother and he could see the fear in her eyes. Would they be delayed so long that they missed their flight to Boston? How long would they have to stay here? They wouldn't, couldn't be sent back to Lebanon. Could they?

About 100 Lebanese crowded in the small room with walls painted a sickly white. There was a tube light that was about to go out and gave the room an annoying strobe light effect.

"All U.S. visa holders must have this background check application completely filled out." The redhead held a piece of paper above his head indicating what none of them had either seen or heard of. Abraham looked at the man on his left who was pressed up against him in the crowded room.

"Did you hear of any background check when you went to the U.S. embassy?" he asked the man, who was about Elias' age.

"I barely got my visa," he replied. "The embassy was a madhouse when I went. Everyone wants out."

"Give us your copy and we'll fill it out," someone said from the midst of the crowd.

"I'm not a copying service. The U.S. embassy here says you go nowhere without this document."

This declaration caused the murmur to become a dull roar.

"Excuse me!" Maya declared in a tone that caused the crowd to quiet. "We have been in an airplane for six hours. I need to use the bathroom. Then we can talk about this background check."

The redhead could not stand in the way of 100 Lebanese who clearly needed a bathroom break.

"OK. Outside the door and to your left are bathrooms. But don't go too far."

Maya now turned to Abraham. "Call your father."

Abraham found a pay phone and pressed zero. The operator answered in French, which was a relief to Abraham as he didn't know any German.

"Je voudrais placer un appel téléphonique à Boston," Abraham told the operator.

"Quatre francs s'il vous plaît."

"Hold on." Abraham dropped the phone.

He looked left and right. He saw an older man walking with a cane. "Excuse me, do you speak English?"

The man shook his head.

"Parlez-vous français?"

"Oui."

Abraham then explained hurriedly that he needed to call his father and needed four one-franc coins very badly and he pulled out one of the $20 bills he had taken out of his father's bank in Beirut for an emergency such as this.

The man reached into his pocket and counted out five one-franc coins into Abraham's hand. Abraham tried to press the $20 into the man's hands, but he pulled them back and waved them rhythmically in the space between his head and Abraham's.

"No, my son," he said in French. "I was once a young man in difficult circumstances myself."

"Merci," Abraham said, holding up the coins. "Merci beaucoup."

He returned to the booth and picked up the receiver he had let hanging by its metal cord, "Hello? Hello?"

"Please insert four francs," the French-speaking operator had, miraculously, held the line.

With the money inserted and the connection made, he could only hope that his father was at the home he was sharing with his brother-in-law. As the phone rang, he looked at his watch. It read a quarter past five and he anxiously scanned the walls of the lobby as he had no idea what time it was in Geneva. When he spotted the clock over the money changing booth, he was stunned to find that it was a quarter past four. He felt like he was a world away from Beirut, but he had only traversed one time zone. It must be something like midday in the U.S. but he hoped his father was there.

"Hello?" The voice on the other end was that of his Uncle Michael. It had been many years since he had spoken to him, but he knew his voice immediately.

"*Khalu?*" Abraham said, using the Arabic word he had addressed his uncle by since he began speaking.

"Oh, Abraham, so good to hear from you. I imagine you are making your connection in Geneva. Is everything going okay?"

"Not so much. Is father around."

"Oh my. Yes he's downstairs I believe. I will get him."

For a few anxious moments he could hear Michael calling after his father. Then the familiar voice came over the receiver.

"Hello, Abraham? Your uncle said something is the matter?"

"*Baba*, they are saying we need to have a background check application to continue to the U.S. I have never heard of such a thing or seen it."

"Okay, okay, calm down my son."

There was again a pause while Elias and Michael talked. Just then a voice came over the intercom: "Passengers of SwissAir flight 105 who are connecting to U.S. destinations, please return to security room 12 in the international terminal."

"*Abi*, I have to go."

"Okay son, we have an idea, but it may take a few minutes. Try to stall as long as you can."

Abraham had no idea what they could do in such a short time. He began to imagine the worst. What if they were forced to return to Beirut? What would happen to Ringo? Though it might seem like the most trivial of concerns, Ringo was one of his few connections to Leyla and he couldn't bear the thought of losing him.

Amid the flow of people returning to that bare room with the flickering fluorescent light he spotted his mother.

"Did you get him?" she asked while looking straight ahead as they passed through the doorway to the cramped space.

"Yes. They say they are working on something."

She looked at him and he could read in her face the same thing he was wondering. What could they possibly be working on?

The stern security officer stood at the front, this time accompanied by what looked to be an American diplomat, an older woman with hair drawn back into a bun and wearing horn-rimmed glasses that even in the Arab world passed out of style 10 years previous.

"This is Margaret," the guard began. "She represents the U.S. consulate here in Geneva. She assures me that anyone who does not have their completed background check form will not be able to leave Geneva until the form is complete. If you do not have the form, you will have to clear customs here in Geneva. We have contacted the Red Cross and they have prepared a temporary shelter for your use. Your baggage will be forwarded there at a later date."

A murmur again went through the crowd.

"Who will reimburse our tickets?" someone asked. "I have a job that starts next week," someone else interposed.

"Everyone follow me. I will take you to the Red Cross representative."

Margaret pushed her way through the crowd and out the door and began leading the way out of the cramped space.

"Wait, I have to use the bathroom." Abraham knew it was a poor excuse but it was the only one he could think of.

Margaret turned around and peered at Abraham over her horn-rimmed glasses, looking every bit the dowdy schoolmarm.

At that moment Abraham was startled by the sound of a phone ringing. He had not noticed that in the back of the room, posted on the wall was a telephone. Each time it rang, a red light added to its hue to the dull, pulsating blue hue of the sickly fluorescent light.

The Swiss security agent, seemingly also startled, gathered himself to answer.

"Yes, this is Kraft. ... Yes ... Yes ... Okay."

He raised the phone above his head. It's the embassy in Bern.

Now the look of concern passed from many Lebanese faces to the one American face. She again pushed her way through the crowd, this time to the back of the enclosure. She took the phone from Kraft's hand.

"It's the ambassador," he said ominously.

"Hello Nate. You need to speak to ... Oh ... uh huh ... but you had sai... okay okay ... I'll do it, but don't send me on one of these expeditions again."

She hung up the phone firmly and turned to address the crowd.

"I understand we failed to give you the form when you visited our Beirut embassy."

Now Abraham finally found the courage to speak forcefully.

"That's what we have been telling you and this guy for the last half hour, but no one would listen."

"Well, evidently someone is now. You have permission to head to your final destination. We will do the background check when you reach the U.S. You are dismissed."

And with that she pushed her way back through the befuddled crowd and out the door.

Abraham sensed that his father or, more likely, Michael had something to do with this, but he had no idea what. Had his uncle become so well connected in such a short time in the U.S.? If so, they should have no problems in their new country.

He turned to his mother. "Let's go before they can think up another reason to keep us."

The rest of the flight was uneventful. Abraham's heart started pounding as they approached the gate in Boston. Would they again be corralled into a room and asked for papers they had never been given?

When they went through in the customs line Abraham thought his worst fears had been realized. The line he and his mother queued in was overseen by a burly redhead with an accent he was soon to become accustomed to, that uniquely Boston habit of dropping the "r" so that when he was asked for his passport he heard something like "passpaht."

The redhead typed his passport number into the green-screen computer, but was clearly frustrated by the result he was getting.

"Damn thing won't wohk," he muttered, striking the top of the computer with his closed fist, a form of technical support that clearly wasn't working. The redhead pushed his passport and visa back at him, "Please step to da otha side of the line."

"Excuse me, where?" Abraham was quite confused by the accent and couldn't see any line.

"Ova theah!" he snapped pointing at an area set off by yellow tape on the floor.

Maya was next in the customs line and, being told the same thing after the computer again malfunctioned, soon joined her son in the corner of the room. A woman in a blue security uniform walked briskly past them and said "follow me."

They gathered their carry-ons and followed the lady into a room marked "authorized personnel only." When they went in Abraham's eyes filled with tears. Almost before seeing his father, he could sense his steadying presence. It had now been a year since he had seen his father and he looked rejuvenated by his year in the U.S.

"*Abi!*" Abraham exclaimed and he embraced his father.

He almost didn't notice Michael, who at the same time was hugging his sister.

"*Khalu*," Abraham held out his hand to shake Michael's. "Am I to understand that you had something to do with our reprieve at the Geneva airport?"

All this he was saying in Arabic while the uniformed security officer was standing by.

"I don't want to interrupt your family reunion, but I need to check your passport and visa. Our immigration mainframe is down and we're having to check everything by hand. I'll write the information down and verify it when the mainframe comes back up." She ripped a yellow sheet of paper off of a pad and handed it to Abraham. "We'll have to keep the dog in quarantine for 40 days. Then you can come pick her up."

"Him," Abraham insisted.

"Him," the security lady repeated. "You can pick him up in 40 days. You just have to pay a $120 boarding fee."

That was a big sum, but at the moment it seemed to Abraham a small price to pay to be in a safe place, away from the bombs, away from the fanatics, away from the darkness that had consumed Leyla.

That night, July 25, 1977, was a big celebration at Michael's house. Dozens of Lebanese whom Abraham had never met were there. Michael lived in the community of Watertown, a district dominated by white working-class Boston natives, but with pockets of Armenians, Greeks and, obviously, a number of Lebanese. There was even a Maronite church a half hour away in Jamaica Plain where Elias had taken up his volunteer work where he had left off in Beirut.

"Maya, Abraham, remember the Zakaryans?" Elias said, presenting the family of four who had once been the Hajjars' neighbors in Beirut.

"Ani," Maya exclaimed while embracing her old neighbor. "How long have you been in the U.S.? We had no idea where you had went."

"We went to Canada first," Arthur Zakarya explained, "but I had some old business partners in Boston who told me there were both Armenians and Lebanese in Boston, so where else could I go?"

Their sons, Jack and Arthur Junior, were acquaintances but not close friends of Abraham. Now that all three were adults the four and six years they were his senior did not seem like so large a gulf.

"Arak?" Michael offered.

"Sure," Abraham said. He didn't particularly care for arak, a drink with the pungent taste of licorice but none of the sweetness of the candies. In its pure form it is clear but when mixed with water it turned a milky white. Abraham thought that a good metaphor for life, how it starts with so much clarity and suddenly and unexpectedly becomes murky.

"So, *Khalu*, you never told me how you managed to get us out of our predicament in Geneva."

"Actually, my dead dog got you out of your predicament."

This caused a look of puzzlement on Abraham's face, which Michael answered with a business card. It read "Alfred Atherton Jr. Under Secretary of State for Near Eastern Affairs."

"I was a bit too busy to walk Jericho and usually I could let him out to do his business and he would come right back in. Evidently this time he got too far into the street. I knew it was bad the moment I heard it. Fortunately for Jericho he didn't suffer. Anyway, this fellow felt really bad and said if I ever needed anything to give him a call."

"Wow, you used your favor on me?"

"No, I used it for my sister. You just happen to be her son."

Michael smiled warmly and patted Abraham on the cheek.

"Fortunately for you, you look just like her, so I am inclined to take pity on you."

Thus Abraham discovered that the U.S. was not all that different from Lebanon. Being owed a favor by the right person could, even here in the home to one of the world's biggest bureaucracies, makes all the difference.

"So, now that you're in the States, what is your plan?"

"I think I want to continue to pursue computer science," Abraham said thoughtfully.

"Really?" Michael's eyes widened. "I'm surprised. I thought you said you were done with computers."

"If a big government like the US gets screwed up because their computer system is down like happened today, then there is room for improvement and I can help, and make some money doing it."

Michael thought this was the strangest thing he had ever heard, but the more he thought about it, the more it made sense. Abraham was a critical thinker, always finding opportunity in adversity. That is the reason he had survived. The world couldn't bring Abraham down. The only person who could do that was Abraham himself.

# Chapter Eleven

Elias Hajjar had never been the wealthiest of men in Beirut, but he prided himself on self-sufficiency. His income as a vice president of the Beirut branch of the Bank of Paris had given his family a comfortable income and no one in his sphere went hungry, or without needed medical care. Often he was able to give these gifts anonymously, but most around him knew the kind of man Elias was, and, in his heart of hearts, he enjoyed being thought of as benevolent.

Thus, Elias' life in the U.S. weighed upon him heavily. His new bank job, as a loan officer for the Bank of Boston, paid little more than that of an entry-level teller. He was living with and off of his brother-in-law, a fact that was his first thought every morning upon waking and remembering exactly where he was and what life had led him to.

Many a morning Maya saw Elias rise from sleep with a smile on his face, but then turn his head from left to right, losing his smile, taking on a dark, ominous cast when he realized his dreams of Beirut were just that, dreams of a past life now lost.

"What's the matter darling?" Maya would ask. It would take Elias a second to recover the mask of satisfaction he wore most of the day.

"Nothing at all, *habibti*. Go back to sleep. It is barely 6 a.m."

But, of course Maya had to get up soon as well. For the first time in her life she had started working in the hopes of saving up enough to put down a deposit on an apartment, though rent in Boston was unfathomably expensive. Maya had a talent with the needle and had started by sewing a dress for Michael's 6-year-old daughter Lena. Michael's wife Mona, whom Maya had known as a little girl back in Beirut, was reminded of just how talented a seamstress Maya was and she suggested that she take in piece work from the Zakaryans, the Hajjars' old neighbors from Beirut. Maya thought that was a great idea and Ani was overjoyed when she saw her old friend come into their shop.

"It's good for a woman to have something to occupy her hands," Ani told her. "God knows our families occupy our heads."

Another reason for Ani's joy in seeing Maya is that she and Arthur were soon to return to Beirut in order to sell their home and shop. Despite the raging war, commerce and an economy of sorts continued in Lebanon and their property was valuable enough that the proceeds could purchase a modest home in Boston.

Not only would Maya work on alterations, she would help Arthur Jr. look after the shop in the Zakaryans' absence.

"Aren't you afraid to go back?" Maya asked with trepidation, not wanting to stir fear, but incredulous that any amount of money could draw someone back to Beirut.

"No, not really," Ani responded. "What God wills, God wills."

That was a sort of fatalism Maya couldn't afford. To her, her life was what she made it, not what God willed. God had his will, but he had allowed her to have hers as well, and she was going to use it to make sure her family survived.

Elias did not want to think about the fact that his wife was bringing in income. That was his job and not to be able to earn enough to support his family when it consisted of only three people was emasculating.

Elias walked across the upstairs hallway and knocked on the door the Abraham's room.

"Abraham, it is time to get up or you will be late for school."

Every day Abraham commuted 12 miles to the Wilson Valley Institute of Technology, a school that had agreed to accept at least some of his credits from Beirut and where he was in the last year of his computer sciences bachelor's degree.

Abraham was daily reminded of his status as a guest in his new country. As a guest, he didn't want to complain, but many of his fellow students who were natives to Boston, thought it was funny to address him as "raghead" even though he was Christian and never wore a turban.

A relatively friendly guy named Jamie even took to calling him "7-11," a reference to the fact that so many Middle Eastern immigrants worked behind convenience store counters.

After class one day, Jamie offered to let Abraham drive his car while he stayed behind at school.

"You do know how to drive, don't ya 7-11?"

"I've been driving since I was 13," Abraham retorted, not at all amused.

"Really? I thought you guys rode donkeys over there."

At that moment, Abraham had the desire to punch his newly acquired friend in the mouth, but he restrained himself because he wanted the opportunity to drive around town as he had driven around Beirut in his old Austin Cooper.

"Come back and get me at 6," Jamie said as he tossed the Camaro's keys to Abraham. "I have tickets to the Red Sox."

Abraham did not particularly like baseball but he was a guest in this country and this was called the national pastime, but it seemed tedious and lacked the action of his preferred spectator sport, hockey.

Wilson Valley was not in much of a valley at all, up in Melrose. Certainly there was nothing like the hills of Beirut that oversaw the mighty Mediterranean, but there was a bay that led out to the mighty Atlantic Ocean. He drove out to Winthrop, about as far east as you could go and still be in Boston. As he looked out over the bay he watched a plane taking off from Logan Airport, just behind him. In just 10 more days he'd be able to go pick up his best friend Ringo. He recalled times he'd spent like this with Ringo and Leyla, watching the planes leave from Beirut's airport, heading out to points unknown. How he had longed to be on those airplanes, to seek out some new spot and now he was in one and he felt no sense of adventure, no tinge of excitement. He longed to do something now impossible, to go somewhere no plane could take him. To go back and be with his two best friends, one now locked up in a cage and one now dead.

When he arrived back at campus, Jamie had two girls with him and Abraham was immediately shaken.

"Mind if we come along?" said the one with long dark hair, whom he would later learn was named Gina.

"Hey 7-11, why don't you let Gina ride up front with you. I'll be back here with my friend Stacy."

Stacy was a freckled redhead, a complexion that Jamie was especially fond of.

In that moment Abraham thought of the difference between this group and his old crowd — Roger and Raymond, Leyla and Ahmed — people for whom he felt an affinity, with whom he could overcome his natural introversion and experience an almost out-of-body joy. These people felt more like aliens.

"Mind if I sit here?" Gina said as she took the front passenger seat. She pulled on his arm and he reflexively pulled it back.

"What the matter?" Gina said, pouting in an extravagant show of being wounded. She swung her head toward the backseat. "I thought you said your buddy was a fun guy."

"He's the strong, dark, silent type," Jamie said. "Sort of a young Omar Sharif."

"Ooh, you're right. I like Omar Sharif."

At that moment Abraham switched into second gear and the car took off in a lurch. Gina was thrown into the back of her bucket seat and they sped off toward Fenway.

When they got there, Jamie pulled him aside.

"What's the matter with you. Gina is a dark, Italian beauty."

Abraham was silent.

"Oh, you want to switch?"

"No, I don't want to switch."

"Tell me 7-11, are you queer or something. I keep trying to fix you up and you keep dodging me."

"No, I'm not queer and no, I don't need fixing up. I need to graduate and get a job. Then I can worry about finding someone."

"But in the meantime you don't want to have a little fun?"

Abraham hated the cavalier attitude toward life he found in the United States. It was as if things had been so easy for so long that everyone got to take life for granted, that there would never be a bill to pay. Abraham now was mature enough to know that payday would come one day.

When he got home that evening there was a heavy quiet over the upstairs portion of Michael's house where Elias, Maya and Abraham now lived. Abraham could tell his parents had been fighting, a rare occurrence because usually Elias would consult with Maya, then proclaim Maya's determination to be his own, and this became the law of the household. But this time Elias had his own opinion and he was resisting acceding to Maya's wishes.

"Your father wants to return to Beirut," Maya said when Abraham asked what was the matter.

Abraham was stunned. They had worked so hard and Beirut, if anything, was much worse, if the 6:30 nightly news reports read by Walter Cronkite were to be believed. But the more he thought about it, the more the idea made sense. He wasn't fitting in with American society and those whom he might call friends only made fun of him.

It was about this time that Maya became increasingly alarmed that, three months after the Zakaryans had returned to Beirut, it had been three days since Arthur Jr. had received a phone call from his parents. The contacts that he had managed to reach, friends mainly but also a couple of relatives, had not seen them in roughly the same three-day period. Arthur Sr. said that he thought they had reached agreement to sell both the shop and home. He suggested that Junior call the bank that had arranged the sale and when, after much effort, he contacted the bank officer who was in charge the news was even more disturbing. The bank officer said the closing papers had been signed and they had deposited the money with plans to transfer the funds to Boston later. The day before the transfer was to take place, Arthur had come in demanding to take out the cash. That, the bank officer said, was the last time he had seen either of the Zakaryans.

Maya knew from experience what taking out such a large sum of money could mean, after her own husband and so many friends and neighbors had fallen victim to Beirut's hostage takers. The bank officer agreed to send the police, such as they were in the chaos that Beirut had become, over to the Zakaryan house. Just two hours later they received a call from the police chief.

"Hold on," Jack the youngest son, said. "You talk to him Mrs. Hajjar." He held out the receiver to Maya. "You can handle whatever he has to say. I don't know if I can."

Maya felt a calm determination take over and a motherly instinct to protect this young man from whatever had happened.

"Yes, sir, this is Maya Hajjar. I am taking care of Mr. Zakaryan's business interests in the U.S. What did you learn?"

The chief told her that Arthur and Ani had been found dead. Their throats had been slit. Their deaths had likely come three days before, shortly after Arthur had removed $60,000 from his bank account.

She closed her eyes and Jack crumpled behind the counter of the alterations shop while Arthur Junior walked toward the door, locked it and turned the sign so that the word "closed" faced out.

"You will be investigating this?" she asked.

"We will do our best," the chief replied, but Maya knew that any justice was unlikely and that a portion of that $60,000 would end up in the pocket of whatever police detective threatened to reveal the culprit, either that or a bullet would wind up in the detective's head. Perhaps both would happen, but what would not happen is justice for Arthur and Ani.

She thought about her friends, the terror Ani must have felt when she was being held by brutes with a gun to her head, the terror Arthur must have felt as he desperately tried to buy her time by taking the cash out of the bank, cash that was unlikely to save either of their lives, but what could he do? He likely decided he would rather die with Ani than live without her. That was a calculation he must have made because he likely knew her kidnappers — strangers wouldn't know that Arthur and Ani were selling their property and therefore had ready access to cash — and they wouldn't want to leave behind witnesses. But he got the cash anyway, buying more time for himself and his wife. It was the kind of terrible decision that was being made every day in Lebanon.

Maya made the arrangements to receive the remains at Logan Airport and have them transported to the funeral home. Their services were held a week later at the Armenian Orthodox Church in Watertown, their caskets adorned with the cross of Antioch, a symbol with three cross pieces to represent the Holy Trinity, but which also reminded Maya of the cedar of Lebanon, the centerpiece of the Lebanese flag, only with the evergreen stripped from its branches, bare and dying, like Lebanon itself.

"We cannot go back," she said quietly to Elias as they sat next to each other in their pew toward the back of the church while the priest recited the funeral liturgy, waving the incense holder back and forth amid the coffins.

"I know," Elias replied and he said nothing more about going back to Lebanon. Who knows what would become of their property back home, but Elias knew he could not endanger Maya or Abraham in a vain attempt to get some piece of the life they had left back again. For Elias the sadness ran deeper than a monetary loss. Perhaps one day the war would be over and Abraham would be able to return to a different sort of Beirut, one that was revived and bore some similarity to the vibrant place of his youth. But deep in his soul Elias knew that he would never again see his home, that God had fated him to spend his final days in a strange country with strange customs. He wasn't a man given to tears, but inside of himself he wept over the life that was forever lost. When he first got his appointment as vice president of the Bank of Paris, he had purchased a plot of land high in the Mount Lebanon range overlooking the city of Bteghrine in the center of the country. It was a place he had dreamed of retiring, where he would take future grandchildren onto his knee and he would be able to finally rest with his beloved wife.

Elias contacted an old business associate from his bank and instructed him to sell his house in Broumana, a family home he had inherited in the countryside as well as the land that was to be his mountain retreat at whatever price could be gotten and the associate would keep a fifth of the sale price as commission. To Elias' surprise the land and homes sold for a decent price, and the remaining four-fifths enabled him to purchase a nice home in the leafy suburb of Watertown.

# Chapter Twelve

1979 was a year that started out hopefully for Lebanon and for the Hajjars. Bachir Gemayel was building up what looked like a legitimate government in Beirut with U.S. backing. In Boston, Elias and Maya were settling in to American life. Both had gotten their residency and Abraham was well on his way to a computer science degree at the Wilson Valley Institute of Technology. Maya could imagine that things were finally falling into place for them, with one exception. Abraham — who had many friends, many of whom were women — never had a serious girlfriend. From time to time it would be obvious that a particular girl from school would take a liking to Abraham. Abraham was always painstakingly courteous, but he would grow colder whenever he knew a girl had serious interest in him. Once a girl who went to Wilson Valley, a striking dark-haired girl with beautiful blue eyes and whose parents were Lebanese and friends of the Hajjars, asked Maya if Abraham were, perhaps, gay. This was a word that Maya had just become familiar with and that many younger people were using to refer to homosexuals.

"Of course not," she said, in part convincing herself. "He's just a serious student. He's always been serious and he wants to make sure he gets himself well established before starting a family."

Maya smiled warmly at the young lady, recovering her confidence that had briefly faltered. "If you are still available in two years when he graduates, ask him out. I'm sure he'll be interested."

Two years later, after Abraham had graduated and began student teaching in pursuit of his master's, the Lebanese girl did ask, and he wasn't interested.

The night, after the girl had informed Maya of the outcome, she confronted Abraham at the dinner table.

"Abraham, when are you going to find a girl?" It was a question he had heard her ask many times before, though usually with a hint or a hopeful introduction or an endorsement of one or another girl he had in the car with him on the way to some social event.

He sat back in his chair and shot his mother a look of exasperation.

"I'll do it in my own time, my own way," he said in a tone crafted to end the conversation, but Maya would not be so easily dissuaded.

"If you're worried about money to start a home, you know your father and I will help you."

"I don't need charity and I don't need your advice," he said, seeking a way out of the conversation. "Father, will you ask mother to stop hounding me."

"If I had such control over your mother I would have used it years ago to convince her to give me a daughter," he said with a wry smile.

"Mom, I just want to get established and find a nice Lebanese girl."

"What about Miriam? She's Lebanese and you have rejected her twice."

"Mom, Miriam came to this country with her parents at 6. She's as American as apple pie. And what are you doing talking to my friends behind my back," he turned in exasperation. "Father, you see my point?"

"I do," Elias said, wiping his glasses with a corner of his napkin. "It's just that there is nothing I can do about it. If I had power over your mother we would have risked everything and moved back to Lebanon. But your mother prefers a more stable home. That is what she wants for you. I hope that, eventually, you will listen to her. A good woman makes a man. Until you get one, you are still a boy."

Abraham saw this was going nowhere. "I'm taking Ringo for walk," he declared.

By now, the only connection that Abraham had with Lebanon and Leyla was through Ringo. Whenever he took Ringo for a walk, he remembered the old days and he remembered Leyla, and for the briefest of moments it was as if she were back there or, rather, he was back in Beirut with her. Walking with Ringo on the way to the pub to meet friends.

He began to think how nice it would be if she were here with him, that she would not be harassed as she was in Lebanon. Of course, Americans would come on to her as would men anywhere, but she would not be treated like dirt the way she was treated by the fanatics back home. She would love Boston, especially in the fall. She had always remarked on the vibrant colors of fall and how they made her feel alive. If only she had realized that the beauty of fall gives way to the death of winter.

Abraham never made the connection that perhaps his problem with other girls could be due to Leyla. At the time, he hadn't allowed himself to think about a life with Leyla, worried that being something more than friends carried the risk of ending their friendship even if it held the opportunity of something deeper. That instinct, maybe it was a fear, an avoidance of risking something reliable for a chance at something deeper, had come to define Abraham.

He crouched and scruffled Ringo's ears and looked into those eyes and wondered what it would have been like to take this walk with Leyla. At that moment a chipmunk a pair of chipmunks ran down a nearby tree and Ringo immediately went to give chase. As he did, he gave out an oddly hoarse bark that Abraham had never heard before. It had been a couple of years since he had taken Ringo to the vet and he made a mental note that it was time to return.

# Chapter Thirteen

Academic pursuits came easily to Abraham. Unlike people, computers were complex, but predictable. Input results in output. In time Abraham got his master's degree and was given an assistant professorship in the early 80s even though he had only just begun his Ph.D. His colleagues respected him and had no doubt he would succeed. By 1990 he had achieved tenure and a full professorship. From time to time he would work on projects creating code for the newly burgeoning landscape called the World Wide Web. The extra income allowed him to help out his parents. Elias had retired from work at the bank around 1990 and, though Maya still took in alterations almost as a hobby, the income was not enough to maintain a household in Boston. The weight of the years was beginning to show on Elias' now careworn face.

Ringo had suffered a bout with throat cancer 10 years earlier but had responded to treatment. On a routine checkup in 1990, the cancer had recurred in the now-15-year-old dog.

At the vet's office the doctor took X-rays and came back with bad news.

"I'm sorry Mr. Hajjar. Ringo has an advanced case of throat cancer. There is nothing we can do but make him comfortable. I would advise putting him down soon to limit his suffering."

Abraham's eyes filled with tears. "Can I at least have one more day?"

"It's your choice. Come back when you are ready and we'll take care of things."

Outside, under a bright blue sky, Abraham knelt next to Ringo who gazed back at him silently.

"You remember her, don't you?" Abraham asked, forgetting to be self-conscious about talking to a dog in public. Ringo sat and Abraham pulled him close. Though he knew Ringo couldn't live forever, it was still like the last little bit of Leyla was dying. But Abraham realized he was being selfish. He led Ringo back into the vet's office for the last time.

Despite Abraham's professional success he still taught Computer Science 101, Introduction to Computing Principles, the class usually given to new instructors and sometimes even to grad assistants. Abraham enjoyed meeting young students and getting them engaged in computing.

He was calling roll the first day of just such a class in 1995 and, as is common with all classes, was struggling with the names, which hailed from far-flung places — Xiangs and Hongs, Azikiwes and Chaudrys. Each responded with a lifeless "here" as Abraham perfunctorily recited the names to the best of his ability.

As he reached the T's he came upon a name that was unmistakably Iranian, "Mary Tabrizi" he called out. The "here" sounded so familiar it startled him. He was even more startled when he looked in the direction of this "here" and saw a young lady, relatively small in frame, with brown hair and brown eyes that reminded him immediately of Leyla.

After class she approached to ask about the required project at the end of the semester. As she came closer he could tell she was a bit older than your average intro student, perhaps in her late 20s.

"Tabrizi, that's an Iranian name isn't it?" Abraham startled himself by asking such a personal question.

"Yes, in fact I was born in Tabriz. My family has been there for as long as there are records," her response was frank and straightforward and she looked him in the eye without hesitancy or intimidation. Her manner reminded him of Leyla even more than her face. "My parents came to the U.S. last year."

"Oh, I see," Abraham could muster little else to say. "Well, then, good luck."

"Oh, I won't need it. I took this class four years ago in Tehran. I just have to take it over again because there are no records or transcripts from my old school and I doubt if this school would recognize my credits. This will be a breeze for me."

She put out her hand with an easy smile and he hesitantly reached up to shake it.

"See you tomorrow," she said and turned 180 degrees and marched out the door.

Abraham felt as though he had just had a conversation with Leyla's ghost ... no, not her ghost, because there was nothing illusory about Mary's presence. If Abraham were more religious in the Eastern sense he would have come away with the conviction that Mary was the reincarnation of Leyla.

He walked back to his office to unwrap the sandwich he had

brought but as he eased into his chair.

Before he could take the first bite of his sandwich, the phone rang and, a bit irked, he picked up the receiver.

"Professor Hajjar."

The voice on the other end immediately portended something bad. It was his mother, but the voice was almost otherworldly.

"It's your father. He's had a stroke."

By the time Abraham met his mother at the hospital, his father was on a ventilator, unconscious.

Maya's eyes were swollen. "It's been hard on him, these last two decades."

She started sobbing and Abraham tried to embrace her.

She pushed away, "I should have let him go home. He always wanted to see home one last time."

She relented and allowed Abraham to pull her tear-filled face into his shoulder. "By the time the war was over he was in no shape to travel."

At one point that evening Elias opened his eyes slightly and Abraham tried to step into their gaze, but he said no words and Abraham had no reason to believe he comprehended anything or could perceive a final "I love you" in his son's eyes.

At 10:20 p.m. on an October night in 1995 Elias Hajjar died.

The funeral at the Maronite Church was a beautiful affair, full of the music and ceremony of his homeland. Sitting on the front pew he tilted his head into his mother's ear and whispered, "we have to take him home. It was always his wish to be buried in Lebanon, next to his father."

Repatriating a body is no simple affair. Numerous certifications were required to get Elias' remains approved as cargo on a flight to Beirut, but it was the least that Abraham could do for his father.

The airplane landed on a cloudy day at Beirut's international airport. Abraham couldn't help but remember the turmoil of his departure. He was much calmer today. The war had been over for nearly eight years. As he looked out the window he could see construction on a new terminal that was to replace the old one in just a few months. Perhaps Beirut was becoming again the city of his youth, a city of progress and sophistication, of hope and happiness. It had been snowing as they left Boston's Logan Airport but he had stowed his heavy coat and would not need to put it on here, as the temperature was an agreeable 70 degrees outside.

At customs the issue was not their visas but the disposition of Elias' casket. They had arranged for a hearse to meet them at the airport but it had not yet arrived. When Abraham called, the funeral director was apologetic. They had misrecorded the flight Elias would be arriving on. They sat outside the terminal and awaited the hearse while the casket was placed discreetly in a room near the baggage claim area.

"Do you think you will be able to meet up with any of your old friends?" Maya asked.

"I've been able to contact one of them, Hassan. He's going to come to the graveside service. I think he might know where the rest are."

"That will be nice," she paused and looked away. "Do you know where your friend is buried?"

"No."

"Sometime's I wonder. If she hadn't died."

"Mom, it wasn't like that."

"I know. But after she died, you changed. You retreated. Inside yourself. Even if she wasn't the one, she would have helped you find the one. She made you a better man. I'm sorry I didn't realize that at the time."

Abraham's eyes filled with tears and he looked away because he couldn't bear to cry in front of his mother. Thankfully, at that moment the hearse drove up.

The driver and the man with him confirmed they were Elias' family and they retrieved the casket and loaded it into the hearse.

The funeral was packed with people who had known Elias from the Bank of Paris, which in the 1980s had been purchased by the Bank of Beirut. Abraham noted, however, that none of his Muslim friends were at the church, especially Samir, the security guard who Elias had assisted and who had saved Elias' life all those years ago.

"He probably was afraid to come to the Christian section of the city," Hassan said as he stood next to Abraham at the graveside service. "I don't mind coming to the cemetery, but even I am a little wary of coming into a church."

"Isn't the war over?" Abraham asked.

"The shooting has stopped, but the war will never be over for the people who lived through it. The war will be over when we die."

After the service Abraham went with Hassan to a coffee shop in

West Beirut. On the way there, Abraham thought of Ringo, for it was in some of these areas they had discovered Ringo and had walked with him before the dog had a name.

As they sipped espressos in a modern Starbucks-like coffee shop, Hassan brought him up to date on the old crowd. Roger, he learned, had married and now had a family with three daughters. Raymond had fought for the government for five years and achieved the rank of captain. He had suffered a bullet wound in the hip and still walked with a limp. Abdullah, he was not surprised to learn, had become a local politician in the Gemayel government and had been assassinated. As they finished their espressos, Hassan said "Follow me, I want to show you something."

He took him a block away to a local government office, the kind of place where people pay their taxes and apply for business permits. On the wall was a row of photographs of varying quality under which was a placard paying testimony to the martyrdom of the person pictured. Hassan led him to the picture in the middle, a man in a suit who unmistakably was Hussein, the member of the fanatics for whom everyone had the most hope, the man who had interceded with Marwan to prevent him from attacking Leyla in the pub 20 years ago.

Abraham was surprised to read that he was the top commander of the Islamic militants of Shiyah a suburb of Beirut of over 200,000 people and where the militants were the strongest in the country that even the army didn't dare to get in. He didn't die in a battle but in a car bomb, most probably put in place by one of his allies in order to take control.

"And what about Marwan?" Abraham asked.

"He died a dog's death. I heard he led a brigade of men who came to hate him. One night, in a firefight, he was shot in the back."

"Good," Abraham said. And that was the last he would have to think about that human scum.

The next day Hassan arranged for a meetup with Roger and Raymond. Abraham asked about the pub near the old school they had always gone to, but it was no longer there, and neither was the school itself, and neither was their Broumana home. All that was familiar about Beirut was gone, most of it being rebuilt, but in a way that didn't feel the same. The neighborhoods were even more segregated now, by religion and even by nationality. And the multi-ethnic world that Abraham knew in the 1970s was a thing of the past.

The place they met at was not a pub but a restaurant that reminded Abraham not of Beirut but on some American chain restaurant. His friends started talking about the good old times, started making jokes, the same old jokes that they had told 20 years ago and suddenly he realized one important thing. Twenty years ago these jokes would have been amusing, he would react to them. Now they didn't mean anything. It was the same feeling he had when he first went to the U.S., when all the talk and jokes people were making were alien to him, and now the same was true but in a way he never thought was possible. He was the foreigner now, in his own homeland. For the first time he realized that Lebanon was no longer his country, the United States of America was his home. It was time to make it so, to settle in America, to have a family.

On the plane going back to Boston he discussed his plans with his mother who was delighted. Elias had been able to do from heaven what he was not able to do on earth. She already had many candidates in mind.

# Chapter Fourteen

As Abraham looked down the list of students in his CS 102 class he is noticed a name: Mary Tabrizi. It was likely she would be taking CS 102 the semester after taking the intro class, but there were three other sections of the class. Abraham was pleased that she was in his. But is it simply because he reminds him of Leyla? Is it because he is drawn to Mary's own confident spirit? He reminded himself quickly that he is a professor and she is a student and such thoughts are improper.

At that moment his reverie was interrupted by Mary's confident voice.

"Professor Hajjar, I'm glad I'm finally getting to be in your class."

"Oh, Mary, How good to see you."

"I was disappointed you couldn't teach the 101 but I was very sorry to hear about your father."

"Thank you, yes, he was a good man. But he died peacefully and painlessly."

"Well I can't wait to get started on the next semester."

Mary again put out her hand and showered Abraham with the same easy, confident smile she did six months ago. And Abraham again hesitantly reached out to shake it.

Over the course of that semester Mary showed herself to be a promising computer student. Abraham would have her in his class twice before she obtained her undergraduate degree and as she neared graduation she requested he be appointed her advisor, a request that was granted.

Abraham would suggest she take part in the many job fairs held by the likes exploding companies like Microsoft and Dell and Yahoo and Altavista. He advised she stick with the former that had a solid business model instead of companies like Altavista, whose presence was solely on the Internet. It all seemed a little too ephemeral to him.

Mary, however, was insistent that she wanted to do research and to teach, so she went right into the master's program at Wilson Valley. One afternoon she knocked on his door.

"Come in," Abraham said absentmindedly while thumbing through PC World.

"Dr. Hajjar, I hear you have an opening for a grad assistant."

Abraham immediately recognized the voice as that of Mary and looked up somewhat startled.

"Yes ... yes. Simon is doing his Ph.D. at MIT. Why? Are you interested?"

"Well, it's better than working at Target. And I have a feeling I'd learn a lot working under you."

"You'd be doing a lot of my CS 101 lectures and grading papers. Pretty routine stuff."

"Computer Science is all about mastering the routine. At least that's what my favorite professor always says."

Abraham smiled softly at hearing one of his catch phrases repeated back to him.

"OK. You can start at the beginning of next semester."

"I would like to start now," she responded.

"We're in finals. There's no money in the budget to pay until January."

"I'll work for free until then. I'm almost done with my thesis. I want your thoughts. I'll trade you for taking the grading of those finals off your hands."

"You've always been one of my cleverer students."

"'Great. Here it is." She reached into her backpack and pulled out a stack of approximately 50 pages clipped into a notebook. "I'll can give you three days to read it and then we'll meet for coffee and you can give me your opinion."

It occurred to Abraham that if a colleague saw the two of them sharing a table at a coffee shop it could appear to be a date. Then it occurred to him that it could be a date, and that he was not altogether opposed to the idea that it was a date. This was a novel notion for Abraham, because he had always loathed the idea that someone else might think he was in a relationship with a woman, even if he was in fact in a relationship with that woman.

Later that day as he was keyboarding in her information with the college's personnel office he was startled when he came across her date of birth: May 17, 1968, exactly 13 years to the day after Leyla was born. Of course, Leyla would never be older than 21 and Mary was now 32, but the similarities were striking.

Leyla graded Abraham's papers and he read her thesis. It was an impressive description of how voice could be translated into data packets and those information packets could be maximized so that they can be transferred over the internet, a technique that was dubbed "voice over Internet protocol" (VOIP). Aside from a few technical clarifications, he wrote on the last page: "I have nothing to add. You surpass me."

"So, I surpass you," Mary said after taking a sip of espresso. "If I didn't know better I'd say that sounded like flirting."

Abraham blushed, then let out a wry smile.

"It would be if it weren't true. I seriously believe you could work at BlackBerry or Lucent or wherever you wanted. You'd make a lot more than you will teaching."

"Maybe someday. But right now I want to try my hand at teaching. My dad makes plenty of money."

"What does he do?"

"He used to be in the military. He was tasked to keep the military up to date with technological advances. He fell out of grace with the regime when I participated at a demonstration for women's rights at the university. Due to his connections we were able to leave Iran and come back to the US. Others didn't have that chance and ended up in jail. Now he does imports and exports, you name it. He's come to this country and once again made himself successful. I guess he's what you'd call a self-made man times two."

"Are you planning on being a self-made woman?"

"I plan on being a woman. I don't need the pressure of 'making' it," she said with air quotes to emphasize her disgust with the concept. "You know what? You should meet my father. I think he'd like you. We're having a few friends over Thursday. Why don't you come?"

"You mean for Christmas dinner?"

"Oh yes, Thursday is Christmas isn't it? Of course, our family is Muslim, but of course, it isn't Muslim in any real since other than DNA. My father hates religion, calls it the source of all evil in the world."

"Your father sounds like a smart man."

"See, I knew you two would like each other."

They did. After dinner Abraham accepted the invitation from Mary's father Ali to go downstairs and play pool over a couple of beers.

"My Mary seems to like you," said Ali, whose broad, severe face was somewhat softened by a slight smile.

"How can you tell?"

"She's 32 and you're only the second man she has brought home,"

Ali said while lining up his next shot. After pocketing the ball he stood erect and looked at Abraham. "The first was her prom date."

Abraham nodded. "I admire her."

"You admire her brain or her body?"

"Neither. I admire her attitude. She reminds me of someone I once knew?"

"Old girlfriend?"

"Old friend."

"Why isn't this old friend your girlfriend or your wife?"

"She's dead."

"Then why wasn't she?"

"That's a good question. I'll add it to the 14,000 other questions I have about my life." With that he pocketed the eight ball. "Game over."

"Oh, my boy," Ali now placed his hand on Abraham's shoulder. "The game is never over."

Of course the only way he could excuse himself from spending Christmas with his mother and her friends from church was to tell her that he was having dinner with a girl. Once she learned that, she wouldn't have let him stay home if he wanted to. She also insisted that she return the favor and that Mary come to their house for dinner.

"Be wary of my mother," Abraham warned Mary as they neared the door.

"You forget. I am a woman. I know a thing or two about my fellow women," Mary said as she pressed the doorbell.

The door opened and the two women regarded each other and embraced. Abraham stood awkwardly, unaccustomed to being a third wheel at his mother's front door.

As they entered Abraham greeted Ani, a tall, angular woman in her 60s with graying blond hair. She had been his parents' neighbor for as long as they had lived in Boston.

Abraham could not relax throughout the meal, which featured his mother's always delicious roasted lamb. During the meal Maya, Mary and Ani talked breezily about life in northern Iran, her family's heritage, and the atmosphere that forced her family to flee.

The conversation that Abraham feared came as Ani was helping Maya distribute the baklava she had prepared for dessert.

"So, Mary, can you see yourself being married anytime soon?"

"Mom, please!" Abraham had mentally rehearsed his reaction all evening, but when it came out it sounded awkward, like the protestation of a 15-year-old embarrassed by his uncouth parent.

"No, no, it's quite all right," Mary said, laying her hand softly on the top of Abraham's arm. "Yes, Mrs. Hajjar, I think I am at an age when most modern women are thinking of marriage and family. I have my master's, I'm closing in on my Ph.D. and once I'm established I would very much like to be a wife and mother."

"Is my Abraham the sort of man you can imagine starting that family with?" Maya pressed.

"Mom," Abraham interjected with exasperation. "I'm 13 years her elder. It's not fair to ask her such questions. She has every right not to commit to someone she would one day be pushing around in a wheelchair."

"It's quite all right, Mrs. Hajjar," Mary said with a nervous smile. "My father is a decade older than my mother and, at least as far as I can tell, they've been quite happy."

"See there, Abraham, that wasn't hard." Maya's voice now sounded like it did when he was 5 and she had just coaxed him into accepting an unwanted inoculation at the doctor's office.

As Abraham was dropping Mary at her apartment he felt the overwhelming need to apologize.

"My mom is ... how should I say?"

"Like every mother of a son who has ever existed? Don't worry about it. Like I said. I'm a woman, too. We understand these things."

As he watched her walking confidently toward the entrance of her complex, Abraham couldn't help but feel a certain awe of that domestic certitude that seemed to go hand-in-hand with femininity. He felt much more confident writing a book or grading a term paper than he did dealing directly with people he'd known as long as he existed. She had just met his mother and was completely at ease.

# Chapter Fifteen

In the immediate aftermath of their mutual meeting of families, Abraham was somewhat withdrawn, keeping his conversations with Mary professional, mostly revolving around lesson plans and test material. He felt they were respecting each other's space to process what they had experienced, to contemplate the futures that they had so clearly confronted in their conversations — Abraham with Mary's father and Mary with Maya.

Abraham knew inside himself that Mary was right for him. He needed a strong woman, someone who would help him overcome his internal hesitancy, someone whom he could respect mentally and admire emotionally. Her statements regarding the age difference between her own parents helped allay his fears regarding his seniority. He was now firmly ensconced in middle age while Mary, though 32, looked like a vivacious 20-something. He hated the idea that he would be taken for her father or, as he truly was, her professor. But he also felt that age gave a man the maturity needed for a woman to truly respect a man because when a man and woman are the same age, the woman is almost invariably more mature.

After Abraham had arrived at the determination that he would propose, the next issue was one most odious to his sensibilities — how to actually pop the question. He hated the manipulation implicit in creating a fancy show — a proposal on the matrix board of a sporting event for instance. But he also was aware of the fact that a woman's sense of the romantic meant that the circumstances had to be special, well thought-out, not a nonchalant or spur-of-the-moment "will you marry me."

He decided that a traditional path — a meal at a nice restaurant followed by a knee and a ring — was likely the best. So he decided on a French place called La Bonne Entente. He pondered telling her where he was making reservations, but decided against it, figuring she'd know automatically what he was planning.

"You know, I'm impressed with this new student in CS 101. She's one of you?"

"Oh really? She's a genius," Abraham said in a reply that forced Mary to crack a smile.

"No, silly, she's Lebanese. Or at least of Lebanese descent. Her name is Foziah Yazbeck."

"That name indeed sounds like one of us."

"She's already dabbled in coding. I think the 101 is really too simple for her."

"Maybe we could transfer her to an independent study and let her credit on the introductory courses while doing something more challenging."

"My thought exactly," Mary said while gathering the paperwork in preparation for going home.

"So Mary," Abraham said in a tone that made her look up from her paperwork, so clear was it that he had something important, something personal to say. "I was wondering if you were available Friday night."

"Let me check," she said, pulling her BlackBerry out of her purse. "Yes! What for?" she exclaimed before she had even given it a cursory glance.

"I thought it might be a nice evening for dinner, maybe to celebrate the end of the semester."

"Ooohkay, that's not for another week."

"I know, but it's been especially hectic. We haven't had much time to talk."

"Oh, sure, where are we going?"

"I was kind of hoping I could make that a surprise."

"Oh, hmmm." Abraham was rarely this mysterious, but she decided there was nothing to be gained by pursuing the matter further. "Sure, OK. I'll be ready. Seven OK?"

"Yes, quite OK."

That Friday, Abraham showed up at the front of her apartment at 6:40. She, of course, wasn't there so he circled the block several times until, around 6:52, she appeared and looked a bit startled.

"You're never this early," she said while getting in.

"I want to make sure we get there early enough that it is still warm enough to sit on the patio."

She expressed no surprise that the restaurant was so swank. He wondered if she was surmising what was to come.

He reached into his coat pocket as she relished her dessert dish of creme brulee.

"I have something I want you to read."

Her eyes looked up at him while the spoonful of creme brulee was still in her mouth. She slowly cleaned the spoon and lowered it back into the dish.

With a look of solemn importance he pulled a folded piece of paper out of the inside pocket on the right side of his sports jacket. She scanned the paper attentively.

"So, this is quite a proposal."

Abraham could feel himself blushing, starting from his chest, up through his neck into his cheeks. That was not the response he was expecting. His heart began to race. He was sure that rejection was coming.

Seeing his obvious discomfort she turned the paper around so that he could see that he had handed her, not a proposal for marriage but Foziah's written proposal for an independent study project.

"So you took me to this snazzy French restaurant to discuss Foziah's independent study? I must say I'm impressed that she is proposing to organize a coding team, but I'm not surprised. She's a born leader."

He reflexively snatched the paper from her hand.

"Oh that wasn't it?" she said.

His stricken face cracked a smile, then they both gave way to a giggle.

"I imagine you already know what this says," he said pulling another piece of paper, this time from his left inside jacket pocket.

"Probably, but I'd just as soon read the scribblings of your students myself." She took the paper in hand. On it was scrupulous handwriting. Abraham had taken great pains to write in cursive, something he was unaccustomed to but he felt that printing it out would be too impersonal. In that cursive, she read the following:

*"My dear Mary.*

*I know already this is awkward. I am not a writer and not much of a romantic. But I have been so happy working by your side these last several years. I am inspired by your spirit. You never give up when I so many times want to. I admire that among so many other things about you. Your energy. Your style. Your easy-going affinity for other people. These are all things that I lack and I feel selfish for wanting them by my side to make up for my lack. But I do want you by my side, so I am asking you now to be my wife, so I will conclude with those four words that are so oft-repeated as to become trite, but I will repeat them because I can think of no other better ones: Will you marry me?"*

She read silently and then folded the letter neatly and started putting it in her purse then stopped herself.

"I'm assuming this is mine to keep?"

Abraham nodded.

She finished putting it into the inside pocket of her purse then looked him straight in the eyes.

"I have two words in reply: 'Yes, but.' I'm guessing you'll want an explanation. I have one for both words. Which do you want first?"

"Well, I'll start with the 'yes.'"

"Abraham Hajjar, you are unique among men I have ever met. Most who were attracted to me made efforts to get in my bed within the month of dating without exception. You are that exception. I haven't figured out whether it is out of fear or that you are an old-fashioned gentleman. But I don't care. I like it. I like the fact that we are at ease with each other. I like the fact that we can talk about programming and hardware and politics and baseball without getting bored or angry. I like the fact that I look forward to going to work with you and going to meet your family with you and, yes, I even look forward to going to bed with you. So, yes, I will marry you."

"And now the 'but,'" he said with a sigh.

"Yes, the 'but.' Here it goes: 'But not for two years.'"

"Ah, yes, I should have known. That's how long you have left on your Ph.D."

"Well then. Now that that's settled shall we order champagne?"

Now that that was settled, Abraham hoped that his mother would be satisfied, no longer harping on when he would marry, but instead she now focused and all the questions Abraham was not yet ready to answer: What would be the wedding date? (There were many relatives in Lebanon who would have to get visas and make travel arrangements) Where would they live? When would the children come?

As for the wedding date, he and Mary finally settled on one — August 11, 2006 — almost exactly one year after the proposal. The wedding itself would be at the Hajjars' church with the reception at the Boston Iranian Association ballroom.

They again had dinner with Mary's parents and Mary's mom was beside herself with joy. She grabbed her daughter's hand again and again. It was a much more modest ring than Abraham could afford. Neither Abraham nor Mary were extravagant people and neither wanted to draw attention to themselves.

After dinner Mary's father Ali invited Abraham to return with him to their basement and the pool table.

"Have you told Mary about your old friend?" Ali asked as he was racking the balls.

"No, not yet. I don't want her to think she is competing with a ghost. Because she isn't."

"It's just my experience," Ali said as he cracked the cue ball into the pile, scattering balls across the table and pocketing three of them, "that it's best to enter into marriage without secrets. They can become poisonous."

Abraham stood silently while Ali made the next two shots, but missed his third.

"I will tell her," Abraham said as he crouched for his first shot. "It just has to be the right time. Leyla was never my girlfriend, only my friend."

Abraham eyed his proposed shot carefully before striking the ball and hitting his intended target squarely into the hold.

"But in an odd way Leyla is the woman who enabled me to have a healthy relationship with a woman like Mary. I've always just missed in life. This time I'm not going to miss."

Over the next several months Mary still kept her apartment but often stayed over at Abraham's place.

"I'm always talking about my life in Iran," Mary said one evening, her head resting on Abraham's shoulder, her body snuggled against his. "You never tell me much of anything about yours in Lebanon."

"There's not much to tell. I was pretty boring."

"I don't believe that," she said, pulling his face toward her so that he was looking straight into her light brown eyes. "You were a young man in an exciting place that was falling apart all around you. The only thing I know about your escape is that you came back with the dog." She had now raised herself onto her elbows. "What was his name." Her eyes narrowed trying to pull the memory of a stray mention back to her mind. "Rocky?"

"Ringo," Abraham said, a bit frustrated by the direction this conversation was taking. "His name was Ringo."

"Like Ringo Starr? I never hear you listening to The Beatles? Did you like them then?"

"Not exactly. I found Ringo while volunteering for the Red Cross after the war had broken out. A coworker found him with me and named him."

"Was this coworker a girl?"

"No, she was definitely a woman." Abraham pondered where he would go from here. This was an opportunity to let her into his world, the world of Leyla and the school in Beirut and the fanatics.

"Oooh, was this woman your girlfriend?"

"No, just a friend. A friend who liked The Beatles but didn't have room for a dog. Now go to sleep."

Abraham had decided against revealing his past. He told himself perhaps someday he'd tell her about his life, about Leyla, but in reality he knew that he built tombs for his memories, surrounded by concrete crypts. Mary had dug as deep as she could and her shovel had hit the outer wall that protected what was deep inside of him from everyone else. He had lost all that was important to him — Leyla, his father, his life in Beirut, and now he was afraid that if he let Mary in it would let too much darkness out. So, he decided, it was for her good and his that he keep it hidden. Perhaps one day he would have the opportunity to reveal more. That opportunity would never come.

# Chapter Sixteen

The morning of April 10, 2006, dawned brilliantly, a sunrise that Abraham viewed as he finished his morning coffee at a shop on the Quincy Shore he had the habit of frequenting after an early morning run and before heading west to school. The previous night Mary had decided to spend at her apartment. She had several projects to grade and wanted the time alone to do so. They still hadn't decided where to live after the wedding and Abraham imagined it possible that they maintain two residences for awhile for convenience. Wouldn't they, after all, occasionally need their own space? Abraham knew he would.

As Abraham was downing the last sip of coffee and pulling on his jacket to head to his car and back to school, a man named Mario Lanpim was walking the halls of the computer science department at Wilson Valley. He noted that about half of the students were female, a higher percentage than other computer science departments he had scouted out around the city.

It would later be pondered why Lanpim, who clearly carried a grudge against women, would have chosen a computer science department when there were many other fields where women were in the majority — a teacher's college, perhaps, or an art school. But later many who studied the case would surmise that Lanpim had felt that women in this field were probably leaving their rightful place in society, taking over a field that should remain the domain of males.

As he stared into a classroom, a green-eyed woman waited behind him to enter the classroom, as her first-hour class was about to begin. She was trying to be patient but she was confused as to why this man, who she knew didn't belong in the class, would be standing there.

"Excuse me," she said, losing a bit of patience under the weight of her books. "Are you looking for a specific classroom?"

He turned his head toward her and looked at her oddly, first above the level of her eyes before finally lowering his gaze the catch hers.

"This is the Computer Science Department right." From the structure of the sentence Foziah took this to be a question, although the cadence was that of a statement.

"These are the classrooms. But if you want the administrative offices or most of the faculty, they are upstairs."

"No," he replied dismissively, "I don't need the faculty. This will do just fine."

He left and walked down the hallway, peering into each room as he passed by. Foziah momentarily thought about alerting someone, perhaps security, but she told herself not to be such a worrier, that people scouted out a new school all the time.

As he peered into the classroom at the end of the hallway, Foziah could hear Mary's voice asked, "Can I help you?" as the odd stranger peered.

"No," he said. "Not right now, but maybe later."

And she saw him walk down toward the campus cafeteria. His voice was odd, but then again in computer science you run into a lot of odd characters. She had to focus on her thesis. In 2006, time waited on no man or woman when it came to finding the next big innovation on the Net and she was determined to make her mark.

Down the hall, Mary was a bit more unnerved by the odd man's sudden appearance. His voice was very disconnected and she had just been through a training session on dealing with emotionally disturbed students. But then, much like Foziah, she comforted herself that she was overdiagnosing. If she were to sound the alarm on every strange bird who walked down the computer science halls she would be at the campus psychologist's office daily.

She looked down the rows of students and was pleased that, for the first time since she had been in a computer science classroom, as a student or a teacher, there was a equal number of male and female students. Girls were starting to take their rightful place in the computer sciences, destroying old stereotypes about boys being better at math and logic.

Abraham pulled his car into his place in front of the CS building. As he exited the car he spilled a bit of coffee on his pants. He normally stuck his head into Mary's classroom to bid good morning but in his haste to rush into the men's room and dab off the spot before it stained he rushed right past Mary's room. By the time he got out of the men's room it was time to head toward his classroom for his morning class, which was to last only one hour before he headed up to his office for grading and planning. Mary's first class of the morning was a two-hour session.

The hour passed uneventfully and as he walked out of his classroom he spotted Foziah leaving her first-period class.

"Foziah," he beckoned. "how is that broadband phone call thing working out?"

"It's voice-over-Internet protocol."

"Oh, right, right. You always were one for words. VOIP. It just doesn't roll off the tongue. I think I like 'that broadband phone call thing' better. I think it would sell. And if it does you have to cut me in."

"Actually there are a few particulars I need to work out."

"Well, if you would like to come up to my office to talk it over, I can always send one of the teaching assistants to grab coffee."

"Thanks. I definitely want to talk it over, but maybe later. I told my lab partner I'd meet him in the student lounge."

"OK. Just let me know."

Abraham turned to mount the steps to his office when Foziah called out, "Oh, Dr. Hajjar."

He turned.

"I wanted to thank you and Professor Tabrizi for inviting me to your wedding and I'm really sorry about not RSVPing ..."

"But you can't make it. I understand," Abraham offered.

"No, I totally want to go. I just completely lost the RSVP card."

"Well, consider it sent and I will see you there."

"Thanks." Foziah smiled brightly and her head cocked to the right. She pivoted around on her tiptoes and headed confidently toward the student lounge. It was that confidence that he admired in all the women he looked up to, Foziah, his Mary and, yes, also in Leyla. As he pondered the confident women he had grown to admire he thought about his impending marriage and the hope he held that soon he might even have a daughter who embodied the same confidence.

That moment was actually the first time he had thought about Leyla in, what? a month? That was probably the longest he had gone without thinking about her. But he had also come to the conclusion that it would only be fair to take his future father-in-law's advice. He couldn't marry someone without telling them about the woman that had made such an impression upon him, who had taught him that even though women hold less power in this world they still can be stronger than men no matter what men do to them. He determined within himself that he would tell her the next opportunity he had.

Mary always faced a challenge keeping her students' attention through the second hour of her class. While it gave her the opportunity to explore subjects in detail, the fact of the matter was that the attention span of late teens wasn't getting any longer as the years went by, and the inventions of computer scientists, these Blackberries that were all the rage now, were aiding in the decline of that attention span.

A couple of students had already nodded off and a couple of others were vacantly sending emails, not paying much attention to the lecture when a loud popping sound coming from down the hallway caused them to jerk into consciousness. At first they, like Abraham upstairs thought it must be an explosion of some sort, but it was followed by another some 10 seconds later. That was the bullet that took Foziah's life. Mary rushed to the door, her training on mental illness and the vacant voice of the stranger still ringing in her head. She saw him dressed all in black and carrying what looked like an automatic rifle.

She slammed the door shut and locked it, telling her students to hide. But the door was not made to withstand the onslaught of a madman and the glass was soon shattered and the man reached his arm inside for the door handle. Mary's instincts took over. She slammed his arm down onto the shards of glass and the man screamed in pain. He jerked his arm back and soon he was shooting at the door. Mary stepped back but not before she felt something warm in her waist. She looked down and realized that the bullet had ricocheted off the door and into her hip. She grabbed the wound and at that moment the door was burst open.

Students who escaped would later note the odd fact that none of the students screamed during all this. They all stood in stunned silence, gathering toward the back of the classroom, perhaps hoping to stay out of harm's way and that the gunman would get distracted and go elsewhere. He wouldn't.

"Men over here." He pointed to the side of the room to his right, "Girls over there." He pointed with his rifle to his left side. No one moved for a moment. The young men and women of the classroom looked at each other in disbelief.

"I said GO!" he shouted and by this time the boys moved to the black-clad stranger's right and then took the opportunity to leave the classroom. The shooter didn't seem to care. There were now eight female students left in the class, along with Mary.

Mary began to feel the throbbing in her hip but felt a determination welling up inside of her to save her girls.

"Any of you girls feminists? Huh?"

Several of the girls were sobbing now.

Mary knew that this was her chance. With all the effort she could muster she hurled herself at the gun. The gunman was momentarily knocked off balance. Two girls ran from the classroom. The gunman steadied himself and pushed Mary off of him with the barrel of the gun. She hit the wall in the front of the classroom with a thud.

He turned and shot the third girl who was attempting to leave in the head at point blank range.

"Anyone else care to leave?"

"I'm not a feminist, sir."

"Excuse me, what did you say?"

"I said I'm not a feminist!"

"For someone who is not a feminist who speak very loudly when addressing a man. Learn some respect."

He shot her in the stomach.

By this time Mary had gathered herself and stood up. With all the energy she could muster she said, "I'm a feminist."

The sound was faint and the gunman could barely hear. He turned.

"What did you say bitch?"

"I said," she wavered, barely able to stand, weak and cold from blood loss. "I said I'm a feminist. At this point she lunged at him with all the animal rage in her core. She tried the wrestle the gun from his hand and, while even at her strongest she had no hope of doing that, she did distract him long enough that the rest of her girls who were yet alive, four in all, would have time to get out. The next day, the Boston Globe would carry a story about the heroic professor who with her dying breath was able to save six of her eight female students from the misogynistic shooter.

But it was her dying breath, for as soon as the shooter got possession of his gun, he hurled her backward, this time toward her desk. Then he shot, once through the heart. She slid downward in front of the desk into a sitting position. When she came to a stop her eyes were still open, though fixed and dilated. Though they were staring at nothing, to the shooter it was as if they were staring at him, accusing him for the coward he had been all his life, telling him that no matter how many women he killed that day, he'd never be as strong as they were. With his left leg he kicked at Mary's head so that her body fell forward, the head facing away from the door, her face covered by her long black tresses. That is the way Abraham would find her.

After the shooting in Professor Tabrizi's room, the shooter went into the school's cafeteria and killed five more women — and the one man who dared to try to stop him — and injured 18. He then went into a theater-style classroom where he shot the female student who was defending her thesis in class. He shot and killed three women who were running out of the classroom and he injured 10 more. He went to shoot another girl cowering behind a seat when he realized the girl on stage was gasping for air. She had been shot in the lung but was still alive. He jumped up on stage and pulled a dagger out of his coat and plunged it into her heart. He stood up on the stage, straightened, took a stiff bow, then pointed the muzzle of the carbine at his head and pulled the trigger.

# Chapter Seventeen

Abraham would later realize he had heard all of these gunshots. He would also later read of Mary's bravery and would actually have opportunity to speak to one of the girls in her class.

"Dr. Hajjar, I'll always owe Professor Tabrizi my life."

"She was quite a hero wasn't she?" he said. What went unsaid was "And I was quite a coward."

Abraham wasn't sure what he could have done had he accosted the madman. But hadn't Mary accosted him with nothing more than her small body and had saved the lives of six women. He had done nothing but cradle the body that represented his second life now lost. He wasn't sure he had another one left in him.

At the funeral Ali looked up at Abraham with eyes bloodshot and vacant.

"That other girl, the one you knew. You said she was dead, but you never said how she died."

"Car accident." He lied without a moment's hesitation. How could he tell him the truth. That two women who had touched his life so intimately had both been killed by misogynists. He began to wonder if some demon was following him through life, tormenting him by taking the lives of women whom he'd grown to love, taunting him by using cowards like the fanatics and the gunman, men who got their power through intimidation of those who could not physically overpower them. Abraham felt like a coward, too. No, he didn't kill or bully, but he couldn't protect. He had always felt weak and twice it had been proven to him how impotent he was.

The school remained closed for the next three weeks, during which it wasn't so much that he refused to eat, it's just that the thought never crossed his mind. His mother tried to convince him to come stay with her. She even told him she was frightened living alone and that his presence made her feel safer. This caused him to laugh aloud. How could he make any woman feel safer?

When he returned to work the school organized group counseling sessions and was paying for twice weekly mental health visits.

Stan Mulcahy, a portly computer science professor with a scruffy beard, stopped by Abraham's office.

"We've been missing you at the group sessions." Stan's tone was surprisingly tentative for such an imposing figure.

"Yeah? Well, I've been busy." Abraham didn't look up from his paperwork so Stan tried to get in his field of vision. He leaned over and put his hand on Abraham's shoulder.

"Listen, Abraham. I know how tough this has been."

"Do you, Stan?" Abraham moved backward in his chair, and pulled his shoulder back from Stan's grasp. "Do you know what it's like to be unable to save everything that matters to you."

"Abraham, I lost students too."

"Well I lost my wife!" Abraham screamed this, a fact made shocking by the fact that he rarely raised his soft-spoken voice. Stan looked shocked. "Listen, Stan ..." Abraham, who had stood to scream, slowly lowered himself back into his swivel chair. "I'm sorry. You don't deserve that. It's just that I can't bring myself to be public about this. Maybe you can. But I can't."

"You are a quiet man Abraham," Stan was again trying to enter the field of vision of Abraham who was staring at the floor. "But you need to be able to talk about this. You can't keep it all inside."

"That's just it Stan. I have kept it all inside. This has happened to me before and I couldn't even bring myself to share that fact with the woman I love. And now I'll never be able to tell Mary. I'll have to live with that for the rest of my life."

"This has happened to you before?"

Abraham sighed heavily. Stan was a harmless, likable colleague. He was as good a person as anyone to tell.

"You know that my family fled the civil war in Lebanon?"

Stan nodded slightly.

"Well, I know you know the history of what a bloody thing it was. But I don't think you could ever comprehend the inhumanity of it. It really turned people into animals, people who otherwise would likely have just been your classmate, your colleague, your neighbor. Lebanon was a progressive society, we had pubs and wine bars and art and music. And there was even a progressive attitude toward women. There was one young woman in particular who embodied the sort of place that Lebanon could become. Her name was Leyla and she was my classmate in computer science at Beirut University."

Stan seemed to start to ask a question, but thought better of it and her and sliced her throat."

Abraham's face contorted and his eyes filled with tears.

"I don't believe in reincarnation. I don't actually believe in much anymore, but if I did, I would say this shooter that took Mary, he is like the reincarnation of those fanatics. They could not stand the existence of self-sufficient women."

A thought occurred to Abraham that made him smile through his tears.

"You know Stan, it just occurred to me what the difference between me and the fanatics, between me and that shooter is. We are all, every one of us, cowards. But I admired those women I met who knew what they wanted in life and pursued it without apology. Those men, those petty tyrants with guns and knives instead of dignity and courage, all they wanted to do is destroy those women."

Over the next few weeks Abraham alternated between throwing himself into his teaching and not being able to get out of bed the entire day. Maya implored him to take advantage of the counseling Wilson Valley was making available and, short of that, allowing her to make an appointment for him with a friend of theirs, a psychologist who attended their church. Finally he relented and allowed her to make the arrangements.

On the day of the appointment he drove his mother's Cadillac Escalade to the Cambridge office of the psychologist in question. Maya's eyesight was worsening and she rarely drove anymore. His mother was quite happy, hoping that this marked a turning point in his life.

"You were always such a sensitive child," Maya started. Abraham could tell she was becoming nostalgic for his boyhood, which usually he hated but now, this time, it didn't seem so annoying.

"Was I mom?"

"Yes you were. Remember when we tried to get you a puppy when you were, what? 7, 8 years old?"

"I was 9, Mom. That dog didn't last two days with us. It ran out in the road and got hit."

"I'll always remember how you cradled that pup in your arms. You were crying and you kept asking, 'Is it hurting? Is it hurting?'" Maya's eyes welled with tears. "You could never stand for anything to suffer, especially something so powerless."

After a long pause she continued. "That sort of sensitivity, it's a beautiful thing. But I know it has hurt you. So much has hurt you."

By now they were pulling into the parking lot of the medical complex. There were no parking spots near to the entrance of the complex so Abraham suggested he drop her off at the door so she could start filling out the paperwork. She agreed. As he pulled the car in front of the door and she started to get out, Abraham felt the sudden impulse to hug his mother. She pulled into his bosom. She was now so frail and thin it almost startled him. It had been a long time since he had hugged Maya.

"I want you to know it's going to be OK," he said. "And I want to thank you for being so supportive. I know I haven't appreciated it enough."

Maya giggled slightly as she emerged from his embrace. "See what I said? You're so sensitive. That's a good thing."

Abraham threw the car into park and ran to the passenger side to open the door and help his mother out.

"Oh, don't bother yourself," she said. "I'll be alright."

He placed his hand on her cheek. "Yes," he said. "Yes you will."

"It's starting to rain," she said. He had hardly noticed the raindrops that flecked his jacket. "You get parked and get inside before it starts to pour."

He watched her enter the building, then got inside and slowly crept forward. Instead of taking the first parking space available, he pulled into a distant section of the lot. He reached inside his left pants pocket and pulled out a box. He then reached into the glove box and fished below the numerous papers inside until he retrieve the small revolver. His mother had likely forgotten she had once put it there when Boston was suffering a summer of unusually high crime. She may not have thought much about it because she had never gotten bullets for it. She had hoped that just having the gun would be enough to scare away a would-be attacker.

Abraham swung open the revolver chamber and carefully placed a bullet in each chamber. He did not have much experience with guns and he didn't want to run the risk of pulling the trigger on an empty chamber.

The rain was heavier now and as the water rushed down the windshield he could only see what was before him through the kept silent.

"No," Abraham continued. "To answer your question she was not my girlfriend. I think that is actually what enabled us to become such close friends. That was never an issue. But make no mistake, I had respect and affection for her like no one I'd known until ... I met ..." He left the word "Mary" unsaid and started sobbing into his hands. Stan again put his hand on Abraham's shoulder and this time the shoulder did not resist. Abraham gathered himself.

"In the same classroom there was a group of students, we called them the 'fanatics,' who had their minds poisoned by the sectarian power struggles going on in Lebanon, always angry, always bent on maintaining the status quo. And the status quo for them meant no women in places where men traditionally walked. And that was dangerous for Leyla. I often think that I should have recognized that and warned her, but then, what could I do? She would never have quit her education. That would be cowardice. She would never surrender her future to those fanatics. Things progressively got worse, in the classroom and in the city. Over time it became clear that the fanatics were going to school for the purpose of becoming weapons system experts for the war that lay ahead. They also became bolder in expressing their opinion, especially their opinion that women didn't belong in the classroom or the workplace."

Stan was looking intently at Abraham. It seemed to Abraham that Stan could see where this account was headed.

"First our professor disappeared. At the time we were unsure as to why but in retrospect I think he was so knowledgeable that the fanatics couldn't risk him working for the other side. He was completely nonpolitical, but he hated the fanatics as much as we did. And of course when I say 'we' I mean our group of friends. Their names wouldn't mean much to you, but they were Roger and Raymond and Abdullah and Hassan. Amazingly of those four, only Abdullah was killed and he wasn't killed in war. He was assassinated while working for the government. The fanatics hated all of us, but they especially hated Leyla, because she was a woman and because she was bright, but mostly because she was independent and if there was anything they hated, it was an independent woman. They left her body in the courtyard of our school, right at the location where we would hang out while eating our lunch. Those savages who pretend to be the defenders of morality had raped

106

distortion of the rushing water. Everything seemed green and black. He turned on the radio, hoping it would somehow distract him and muffle the sound. He thought about what a terrible son he was being, forcing his mother to be alone. But he had always let the women in his life down. He couldn't help any of them. And here was his final failure, his mother. He thought about Leyla and Mary and even Foziah. They were all better humans than was he. All murdered by men.

He wondered if there was some possibility of seeing them. But it seemed to him a faint hope. He had lost whatever faith he had once had. Then he thought of something he hadn't thought about in 40 years. He smiled slightly. It was that French girl to whom he had lost his virginity, how she had put her hand to his lips and said "L'avez-vous pas entendue? Didn't you hear? Don't you understand? Silence!" He didn't understand, but now there would be silence.

The raging of the world would finally stop. At that moment the next song started playing on the radio. It was "It Don't Come Easy," the Ringo Starr song that had inspired Leyla to name their dog. Abraham laughed and looked out the window. The rain had let up and he could see the trees in the parking lot, though the windshield was now becoming fogged by his breath. He placed the barrel of the gun in his mouth.

He was a bit surprised of the coldness of the metal on his lips. He pondered how this was likely the last sensation he would ever have. Coldness. The world was cold. He had grown cold. All the warmth had been taken out of his world by a knife, by a bullet, by a man. He tried to pull the trigger, but he couldn't, there was somebody who would not let him commit suicide, he tried again and again and he was not capable of ending his life, and the thought of being a coward came again into his mind, the one thing that should be easy to do and that he wanted to do he was unable to do. He wasn't able to end his life to join Leyla and Mary.

While he was struggling with his thoughts, he saw the picture of his father, Elias, on the dashboard where his mother always kept it. In the picture his father had piercing eyes, looking at him angrily, something he never noticed before, and he decided that he could not kill himself in front of his father. He put the gun back into the glove compartment, opened the door and walked away. He was never seen again.

www.ingramcontent.com/pod-product-compliance
Lightning Source LLC
Chambersburg PA
CBHW072010170626
46813CB00005B/2102